Arthur Crowther, Thomas Vincent

Jesus, Maria, Joseph

The devout Pilgrim of the ever blessed Virgin Mary

Arthur Crowther, Thomas Vincent

Jesus, Maria, Joseph
The devout Pilgrim of the ever blessed Virgin Mary

ISBN/EAN: 9783742823540

Manufactured in Europe, USA, Canada, Australia, Japa

Cover: Foto ©Andreas Hilbeck / pixelio.de

Manufactured and distributed by brebook publishing software
(www.brebook.com)

Arthur Crowther, Thomas Vincent

Jesus, Maria, Joseph

WE FLY TO YOVR PATRONAGE,
O SACRED MOTHER OF GOD! etc.

FAITH.

HOPE.

CHARITY.

CONFESSION.

COMVNION.

LAST AGONY.

IESVS

JESUS,
MARIA,
JOSEPH:

Or,

The devout Pilgrim of the
ever bleſſed Virgin
MARY.

In his Holy Exerciſes

Upon the ſacred ⎰ JESUS,
Myſteries of ⎱ MARIA,
　　　　　　　 JOSEPH.

With the charitable Aſ-
ſociation for the Relief of
the Souls deparſted.

Publiſhed for the benefit of the pious
Roſariſts, by *A. C.* and *T. V.* Religious
Monks, of the Holy Order of S. *Bennet.*

To her moſt ſacred

MAJESTY,
CATHARINA,
Queen of

Great Brittain.

Madam,

Hat we publiſhed ſome years paſt in a more ample manner, and Dedicated to the Glorious Queen of Heaven; we now in a contracted form, Dedicate to You, the great Queen of this Iſland: And although, ſince your

A 2   happy

happy arrival amongst us,
none (that we know) have
hitherto appeared before
your Majesty with any
presents of this nature ; yet
we hope our being first in
diligence, will not be con-
strued a forwardness of pre-
sumption, but rather (as we
really intend it) the perfor-
mance of a duty ; wherein
we conceive our selves to
stand more engaged to your
Majesty, than many o-
thers ; in regard that our
very subsistence depends (af-
ter God) in a peculiar man-

ner upon your *Patronage*
and *Protection.*

But that which chiefly
both excuseth and encoura-
geth the boldness of this our
address to your sacred Majesty, is the matter and subject of this little Book we
bring; correspondent to its
title of Jesus, Maria, Joseph, *the three lovely names
and objects to which your
solid* Piety *bears so singular
a respect and veneration:*
Piety, *which being thus
strictly allied to your* high

A 3 *place*

place and dignity, and withall tempered with so obli-
ging a sweetness and conde-
scendency, draws a reve-
rential admiration from the
most sensual and insensible
souls : insomuch as even
they who are altogether a-
verse from your opinion in
point of Religion, are ne-
vertheless forc'd to praise
the resolute Piety of your
Devotion; and although
they will not yet brook your
Practise, yet they cannot
chuse but be already in
love

love-with your *Person.*

Now Madam, *since this* your *Piety (though most punctual in the performance of all Religious Duties) seems more particularly eminent in promoting, after* Gods *honour, that of his Holy and Immaculate* Virgin-Mother Mary, *(who was ever esteemed by all* Orthodox Antiquity, *to be the Head-work (next to the sacred humanity of* Gods Son *himself) of all our Creators glo-*

A 4 *rious*

rious products;) as appears
by your singular affection
to the holy Rosary: We
have therefore purposely employed the major part of this
small Treatise, in expli-
cating the Parts and My-
steries of the said Rosa-
ry, for their benefit and
instruction, who are desirous to imitate your Ma-
jesty in this most efficacious manner of Prayer, so
highly priz'd by our Pre-
decessors, and so profitable to all such as with
right

right Intention, sincere
Humility, and fervent
Devotion, will be pleas'd
to make use of it.

And the expectation
of this great profit, gives
us good hopes of your
Majesties gracious accep-
tance of this our mean Oblation, which we accom-
pany with our constantly
continued Petitions to the
Throne of Mercy for your
Temporall and Eternall
Felicity; these being the
best and only proofs we
can

can give of our perpetuall
gratitude, and of the high
and hearty respects of,

Madam,

Your most humble,
most obedient, and most
faithful Servants, Sub-
jects and Chaplains at
the sacred Rosary-Altar,
A. C. and T. V.

AN
Advice to the devout
ROSARISTS.

WE here present you (most dear and devout Brethren and Sisters of the sacred Rosary!) with an iterated Edition of our former *Jesus, Maria, Joseph*; wherein if we have left out some things which were convenient for your instruction, yet surely we are confident to have omitted nothing which is necessary for the daily practise of your devotion; so that it

will prove (as we conceive)
not much lefs profitable, and
yet much more portable than
the former; to which you may
notwithſtanding have perpetual recourſe upon all occaſi-
ons, when you deſire a more
ample explication of the ſacred Myſteries, a more particular examination of the Indulgences, or a larger dilatation of your Affections. And
we have (in lieu of what is
here left out, made an additi-
on, (which vve doubt not will
be moſt grateful unto you,)
of that pious *Aſſociation for the
relief and aſſiſtance of the poor
Souls ſuffering in Purgatory*, as
you ſhall find it deſcribed in
the end of this New Impreſ.

In summe, we doubt not, but *this* will both excuse us, and satisfie you ; that we have proceeded herein (as we hope) according to right reason, as well as with mature deliberation : For since we took up the resolution of presenting this Book to our gracious *Queen Catherine,* we having nothing else whereby we could better testifie our gratitude for the great favour of her protection than a Treatise of the sacred *Rosary,* to which her Majestie is singularlie devoted, (*We tell you, O Rosarists! of this her devotion, for the comfort and encouragement of yours ; and we propose her to you, for a Pattern worthy*

your imitation;) it ought rather (if the mean we aym at
cannot be attained,) to be
too compendious than over
tedious.

Now for that this *Abridgement* will probably fall into
the hands of some who have
not seen that larger explication; it is thought convenient
to transferre from thence hi-
ther these few notes, as seem-
ing to be very useful for each
Rosarists edification and instruction.

*1. Concerning the Title of our
Blessed Lady of Power.*

This is the Sir-name (if
we may so phrase it) of our
sacred

sacred *Altar of the Rosary* : And (amongst the many Titles which are in several places attributed to the sacred Virgin-Mother, according to the several dictamens of each devout Assembly, as *of Pity, of Vertue, of Grace, of Comfort, of Mercy, of Deliverance, &c.*) We made choice of *this Title* as the most glorious, of *this Quality* as most capable to call, invite, and encourage all people to fly to her patronage, of *this Name* which only pronounced cannot choose but afford present comfort: wherfore in all your dangers, difficulties, and distresses, think upon your *Mother of Power*, (O devout Rosarists!) call
upon

upon your *Mother of Power*;
Let her not (*saies a holy Father*) depart from your
mouth, let her not depart
from your heart, calling upon
her you despair not, thinking
upon her you erre not; she
holding you fall not, she protecting you fear not, she guiding you faint not, &c. How
properlie then, (O children
of *Mary!*) do we entitle our
Mother *Powerful,* since (saies
our learned and devout Doctor *Damian*) the Almightie
hath so highlie priviledged
her with all Power in Heaven and Earth? And therefore, be sure(with our mellifluous St. *Bernard*) to deposite in *Maries* hands whatso-

ever you desire to offer up to the divine Majestie, that so your oblation may ascend to the source of grace by the same channel whereby Grace descended unto you, &c. And (concludes this devout Father,) since your all-powerful *Creator* hath in mercie provided this powerful help for you, take special care to place in *Maries* powerful and grateful hands whatsoever petition you desire to prefer to her divine Son, if you would not have it to miscarrie and receive a denial.

2 *Of the Antiquity of the Rosary.*

Though the general devotion of all faithful Christians towards the sacred Virgin *Mary*, is as ancient as our Faith and Christianitie themselves, (she being constituted the Churches Mother by the bequest of her blessed Son, when he uttered those words to St. *John* (as his last Will and Testament) on the Cross, *Son behold thy Mother;* Nor did ever yet any true Catholick, acknowledging *God for his Father, and Christ Jesus for his Brother, exclude* Mary *from being his Mother* : Yet this particular manner of honouring her, this pious method of praying to her, this Confraternitie of the sacred *Rosary,* had its first institution from the glorious St. *Dominick* above four hundred years since, and its decayed use was zealouslie renewed by the blessed Father *Alanus de Rupe,* two hundred years past: For though our glorious Father St. *Bennet,* (as the said *Alanus* relates,)that most worthy Patriarch of Monks, chose the Psalter of the Blessed Virgin for his familiar and perpetual companion, and so deserved to become the famous Founder of Monastical institution, (as *Bucelinus also in his Menologium largely demonstrates,*) yet we pretend not to make him the Author of the *Rosary,* according to the sacred method as it is now recited; No,

This praise belongs properly to the bleſſed St. *Dominick.*

3. *Of the excellency and Utility of this Inſtitute of the Roſary.*

Firſt, It is of that *large extent*, that it hath ſpread it ſelf over the whole habitable World, and acknowledges no other limits, than thoſe which bound the univerſal Church.

Secondlie, It is of that *generality*, that no perſon is excluded from its participation; not the *Husbandman* in the fields, not the *Tradeſman* in his ſhop, not the *Traveller* in his journey, not the *Unlearned* for his ignorance, not the *Woman* by her Sex, not the *Mar-*

ried by their state, not the
Younglings by their simplici-
tie, not the *Aged* by their im-
potencie, not the *Sick* by their
infirmitie: brieflie, not any
devout and *faithful Christian*
by any calling, or condition
whatsoever.

Thirdlie, It is of such *easi-
ness* to learn, and *facility* to
practise, as that it requires no
more knowledge than meer-
lie the skill to recite the *Pater*
and *Ave*, no more expences
than the price of a *pair of
Bedes*, no other place than
where each person lives, no
other posture of the body
than that in which devotion
finds us, whether it be standing, sitting, lying, walking, or

Fourthly, It is of that infinite *Spiritual profit*, that it is impossible in few words to be expressed : *First*, in respect of the special Patronage and Protection of the blessed Virgin. *Secondly*, in respect of the Community of merits, amongst the members of this sacred Rosary. *Thirdly*, in respect of the vast treasure of *Indulgences*, Pardons, Iubilies, *&c.* given and granted (by the prime Pastors of the Church, the general Dispensers of Divine Blessings, the universal Stewards of celestial riches,) to this our holy Confraternity : *Indulgences*, so authentical, as no Catholique can deny them or doubt of them ; so ample, as no association ever had larger ; so many, as to mention them would make up a volume ; there having been scarcely any Pope since *Urban the Fourth*, who hath not freely opened the Churches store-house, and added new favours to his *Predecessors* liberalitie; insomuch as there are extant above forty authentick Instruments issued forth of that highest spiritual Court for the approbation, confirmation, and ornament of this our Confraternity. *Fourthly*, in respect of the confidence and comfort in the article of Death, *&c.* with many other spiritual profits, benefits, and blessings which

accrue.

accrue to you (O devout Rofarifts!) by your being faithful members of this facred
Confraternity: And all thefe
are great helps *to live well and
dye well*, which is the happinefs we all aym at; and for
the obtaining of which we
will pour forth our hearty
and dayly prayers at this facred Altar both for our felves,
and for you; our *devout Brethren and Sifters of this renowned Arch-Confraternity of the
holy Rofary.*

The

The Festivities of our Bl. Lady, according to the monthly days upon which they are celebrated.

JANUARY 22.

THe Feaft of the Espoufals of the facred Virgin Mary to St. Joseph; inftituted in France by Petrus Auratus, of the Holy Order of St. Dominick, who compofed the Office of this folemnity, in the year, 1546.

FEBRUARY. 2.

THe Purification of the facred Virgin Mary, cad'd by the Greek Church, Hipapante Domini, or the meeting of our Lord and his holy Mother, with the Prophet Simeon, Anna, and others in the Temple of Jerufalem upon the fortieth day after his happy birth into the world: where H E was prefented to his Eternal Father, and S H E was purified according to the Law of Mofes, Lev. 12. 6.

MARCH. 25.

THe Annunciation of the moft Bleffed Virgin Mother of God. A Feaft
of

of a great Solemnity and antiquity in the Church, (as appears by the Orations and Homilies of the Primitive Fathers had upon this day;) *in memory of that happy Embassy brought down from heaven to holy Mary, by the Archangel* Gabriel, *in which sh: was denounced and declared Mother of the Word Eternal, and Incarnate,* Luke 1. 31.

MAY 13.

AT Rome, *The Dedication of the Church of Sancta Maria ad Martyres, which Pope* Boniface *the fourth (cleansing the ancient Temple Pantheon consecrated to all the gods) dedicated to the honour of the ever blessed Virgin-Mother, and all the holy Martyrs in the year,* 609.

JUNE. 18.

THe *Feast, or Commemoration of the Psalter of the sacred Virgin* Mary; *appointed by the admirable Father and Patriarch of Monks,* St. Bennet, *to be observ'd in his holy Order; and afterwards propagated by his Disciples throughout the whole world: whereof,* Blessed Alanus de Rupe, *(the great Secretary of the glorious*

Virgin-Mother, and another *Reſtorer* (after his *Father,* S. Dominick) *of this Ma-*
rian Pſalter) hath theſe words; (Apolog.
part. 1. cap. 8. and part 2. cap. 2. 4.) S.
Bennet, *the famous Patriarch of Mona-*
ſtical Inſtitution, introduced the uſe of the
Marian Pſalter (*which he himſelf had*
long before practiſed) amongſt *his Reli-*
gious children; and this not ſo much by
any precept, as by the very uſe thereof
paſſ'd to poſterity as a moſt pious and religious cuſtome.

JULY. 2.

THe *Viſitation of the Bleſſed Virgin*
Mary; *in memory of her viſiting* S.
Elizabeth, *after ſhe had conceiv'd the*
Son of God: at whoſe preſence S. John
the Baptiſt *leap'd in the womb of his Mo-*
ther Elizabeth, *Luke* 1. 41. *which Feaſt*
was inſtituted by Pope Urban *the ſixth, in*
the year 1385. *and promulgated by his ſuc-*
ceſſor Boniface *the ninth, in the year*
1389. *to implore the Bleſſed Virgins aſſi-*
ſtance *againſt the Schiſme which then*
miſerably divided the Church.

AUGUST. 5.

Snow, which miraculously covering a part of the Exquilin mountain neer Rome, at this time when the greatest heats use to parch the City: gave occasion to the building of a famous Church to the sacred Virgin-Mo hers honour (thereby to perpetuate the memory of so signal a miracle) in this same place thus by her self designed, in the year, 367.

15. *The* Assumption of the most sacred Mother of God; *celebrated time out of mind, with greatest solemnity, both by the Greek and Latin Church, in memory of her being assumpted or taken up into heaven, both body and soul after her dissolution.*

SEPTEMBER. 8.

THe Nativity *of the most Blessed Virgin Mary, Mother of God: celebrated both by the Greek and Latin Church, in memory of her happy birth, by* whom *the holy author of all life was born into the world, ever since the Council of* Ephesus, (*which was held in the year* 436. *against the* Nestorians, *denying her title of* Deipara, *or Gods Mother.*)

OCTOBER. 7.

THe *Commemoration* of Holy Mary of Victory *inſtituted by Pope* Pius *the fifth, in memory of the ſignal Naval Victory gain'd by the ſacred Virgins aſſiſtance, this day over the Turks, in the year,* 1571.

Which ſolemnity, was afterwards decreed (by Pope Gregory *the thirteenth) to be yearly celebrated upon the firſt Sunday of this Month, and under the name and Title of the* Feaſt *of the* Roſary, *in the year,* 1573.

NOVEMBER. 21.

THe *Preſentation* of the Bleſſed Virgin Mary in the Temple of Jeruſalem ; *where in her tender age ſhe vow'd her ſelf to God both body and ſoul. Which Feaſt was anciently celebrated in the Greek Church, as appears by the Orations and Homilies of the Grecian Fathers, related by* Surius, *and introduced into the Latin Church by* Nicholas, *the French Abbot, in the year,* 1373. *and afterwards generally received.*

DECEMBER. 8.

THe Conception of the glorious Virgin *Mary* Mother of GOD. A Feast anciently and solemnly celebrated in the Greek Church, and introduc'd into the Latin Church, by S. Anselm Archbishop of Canterbury, in the year, 1106, and commanded to be generally celebrated by Sixtus the IV. in the year 1466, in memory of her miraculous and immaculate Conception by her old and barren Parents, S. Joachim, and S. Anne, and of her being sanctifi'd in the womb, from the first instant of her Conception.

18. The Feast of the Expectation of our Blessed Lady; or the O; Instituted by S. Ildephonse, out of his extraordinary affection and devotion to the Virgin-Mother, and lately approv'd and confirmed by Pope Gregory. 13.

Besides the Festivities of the sacred Virgin-Mother, affix'd (as above) to certain days of the year: there are yet some others which are moveable.

1. UPon the Friday before Palm-Sunday. The Feast, or Commemoration of the sacred Virgins sorrows,

which blessed Simeon prophecied unto her when she presented her Son *Jesus* to his *Eternal Father* in the *Temple*; This Feast is celebrated by the *Cistercians* (as appears in their *Breviary*) upon the 16. of *April*; but by others (more properly) upon the *Friday* before *Palm-Sunday*, in memory of the many swords of sorrow, which pierc'd her maternal heart in her dear Sons *Death and Passion*: *Cardinal Berulle* calls this *Feast*, Festum Dominæ nostræ de pietate; who also composed a particular office of the same.

2. *Upon the Saturday after the Ascension*: The Feast, or Commemoration of the Blessed Virgins Joys, which she receiv'd both in this world, and possesses for all *Eternity in Heaven*: which *Joys* are express'd in most pithy and pious verses, by the glorious *Martyr*, S. *Thomas Arch-bishop* of *Canterbury*, As may be seen in *Canisius*, lib. 4. cap. 13. and which were revealed to S. *Mechtild*, in the first Book of her Revelations, chap. 66.

3. *Upon the last Sunday of August*. The Feast, or Recollection of all the Feasts of the sacred *Virgin-Mother*; which is solemnly celebrated at *Doway* upon this day; though in other places it is transferr'd to the first *Sunday* of *September*. The Institution whereof is

related by Lipſius, lib. 1. cap. 5. de Lova-
nio: and the Office thereof may be found
in the Cambray Breviary, *Printed at Pa-*
ris, 1507.

4. *Upon the Sunday within the Octave
of the Nativity of the Bleſſed Virgin, the
Feaſt of her glorious Name* MARIA,
is with great ſolemnity celebrated at Brux-
els, *and in other places.*

SECT.

SECTION I.

Elevations to the Sacred Trinity upon Earth,

Jesus, Maria, Joseph;

In honour and homage to the Glorious Trinity in Heaven, the Father, Son, and Holy Ghost!

 Jesu, Son of the Living God, and Saviour of the World! O Mary Mother of Jesus, and Mediatrix of Mankind! O Joseph, Bridegroom of Mary, and esteemed Father of Jesus! O sacred Trinity, Jesus, Maria, Joseph! I honour you, reverence you, and prize you in your excellent, eminent, sublime Greatnesses, in which you seem to be an express Image of the Incomprehensible Trinity: And I adhere to you in union of the perfect homages which you rendred to the Father, Son, and Holy Ghost, by your high Estate, and holy

The deep Mystery of the divine Trinity, is Invisible to our eyes, Ineffable to our Tongues, Incomprehensible to our Spirits; And behold, the poor *Bethleem* stable, affords us a humane Trinity, *Jesus*, *Maria*, *Joseph*, upon Earth; which views, adores, and imitates the Trinity of the Empireal Heaven; the Father, Son, and Holy Ghost. *This*, is increated; *that*, is both created, and increated, in the Person of the God Man *Jesus*. *This* is divine, and Eternal; *That* is Deified and temporal. The *one* is adorable; the *other* honourable. The *one* is admirable in its greatness; The *other* amiable in its sweetness. In the *one*, is a Unity of Essence in a Trinity of Persons: In the *other*, is a union of Love, of Grace, and of Spirit, in a Trinity of Essence and of Persons. In the Divine *Trinity* the Father begets his Son in Eternity; In the *other*, by a reverted order, the Son gives Being in Time, both to the Father, and to the Mother. In the *first*, the Father and the Son, and the Father by the Son, produces the Holy Ghost in unity of origin; In the *second*, *Jesus* and *Mary*, and *Jesus* by *Mary*, gives the Life and Being of Grace to *Joseph* in the unity of spirit.

So that *Mary* hath an admirable resemblance to the Eternal Father ; the Son of *Mary* hath an express unity with himself ; and S. *Joseph* represents the Holy Ghost.

For the *Father* in Heaven, is the only Parent without a mother ; and *Mary* upon Earth, is the only Parent without a Father : And as nothing greater can be attributed to God than his being the Father of a God ; so nothing more sublime can befall a pure creature, than to be the Mother of the same God, whereof God is Father.

The Holy Ghost is the sacred knot and Tye of the divine Persons ; And *Joseph* hath a union with *Mary* as his Spouse, and with *Jesus* as his Father : The *Holy Ghost* formed *Jesus* in the Virginal Cloyster of *Maries* Womb ; And *Joseph* fed him, educated him, and preserved for us, (far more fortunately than the ancient *Joseph* of *Egypt*) this Bread of the Elect, this blessed pledge of our future happiness, this Eternal Bliss of Men and Angels.

VVherefore, O *Jesu !* VVe acknowledge, honour, and adore you, In your Eternal heights and greatnesses ; we praise, bless, and love you, in your temporal humiliations and sweetnesses : we

Eye of Faith, between the Father and the Holy Ghost: VVe admire you upon Earth, between *Mary* and *Joseph*; And I invite and conjure all Creatures to praise, bless, and adore your divine Majesty in both these estates.

O *Mary*! We also look upon you, as upon Gods sacred Mother; and in this supream dignity, I salute, reverence, and honour you, with the singular homage of *Hyperdulia*, which is due to your Excellencies and Greatnesses.

O *Joseph*! I likewise honour you, as the reputed Father of *Jesus*, and Bridegroom of *Mary*: And in regard of these two Eminent qualities; I subject my self to the power which is given you over my soul, by consequence of the Jurisdiction you had over *Jesus* my Saviour.

I offer my self to you, O Great Saint *Joseph*, Father, and Husband without Paragon! to be by you presented to *Mary*. I give my self to you, O glorious *Mary*, Virgin and Mother without Parallel! to be by you address'd to *Jesus*. I consecrate my self to you; O Great-little-God-man *Jesus*! as your servant and bondslave, to become associated in this quality, with the domestiques of your sacred Family.

O *Jesu*, my King! reign in my Soul, and exercise the absolute power you have over my spirit. O *Mary*, my Soveraign Queen after my King *Jesus*! possess my heart, and my will, to consign them over to your Son: O *Joseph*, my chief Protector after *Jesus* and *Mary*! take my body and senses into your safe custody, to be consecrated to *Jesus*.

O *Jesu*! annihilate and absorp my soul in your affection; O *Mary*! Inflame my heart with the love of *Jesus*: O *Joseph*! Bless all my labours and endeavours, and present them to *Jesus* and *Mary*.

Let the whole world, be replenished O *Jesu*! with your mercies: be assisted, O *Mary*! with your favours: be secured, O *Joseph*! under the shadow of your Protection.

For, You, O *Jesu*! are the Fountain issuing forth of the Terrestrial Paradise (*Maries* Virginal VVomb) as the Origin of all our happiness: you, O *Mary*! are the Prime Bason of this Fountain, and the pure Glebe from whence it proceeded. And you O *Joseph*! are the River, who disperse abroad these waters of Life by your efficacious intercessions.

O *Jesu*! you are the fruit of life; O *Mary*! you are the Paradise that bore it, and the Tree that brought it forth:

And you, O *Ioseph!* are the Cherubin appointed by God to guard it.

O *Jesu!* You are the sacred *Propitiatory* of the world: O *Mary!* You are the Mystical *Ark* of our Reconciliation. And you, O *Joseph* I are the *High Priest;* who alone are permitted to enter into this Holy of Holies; to be the faithful Coadjutor of Gods great Counsel in the world; and the Feoffee in trust of his treasures and secrets.

In honour therefore of these *three* ineffable Ties and unions between these admirable subjects (which are the greatest under Gods command and Jurisdiction) I most humbly beg of you, O *Jesu, Mary,* and *Joseph*;

1. A chaste and filial *Fear of God*; that nothing, either in life or death, may separate me from his grace and friendship.

2. A faithful, fervent, and persevering *Love* of God and my neighbour, with a generous zeal of the divine honour, and my own salvation.

3. A good and happy *end of my life,* consummated in the act and exercise of these sacred affections.

O *Jesu!* be an Advocate for me your Bondslave to your Eternal Father. O *Mary!* intercede for me your servant, to your Son. O *Joseph!* pray for me your

O *Jesu!* shew your wounds suffered for my sake: O *Mary!* discover your Breasts, which suckled Gods Son: O *Joseph!* represent your hands, which nourished the Word Incarnate.

O *Jesu!* replenish my Soul with the aboundance of your celestial blessings, by the effusion of efficacious grace upon it, which may intimately unite it unto you.

O *Mary!* Poure the milk of your Chast Breasts upon my heart, by the impression of an humble piety and devotion upon it, which may entirely sanctifie my Interiour.

O *Joseph!* bestow on me the blessings of the Earth, (that is, of your labours, sweats, and merits) whereby the works of my hands may become prosperous, and all my exteriour actions, profitable and meritorious.

That honouring and loving you upon Earth, O sacred Trinity, *Jesus, Maria, Joseph!* I may enjoy your happy sight and presence, O *Jesu!* with *Mary* and *Joseph*, in Heaven: and there render due honour, praise, and glory to the *Father, Son,* and *Holy Ghost,* one only God, for all Eternity. *Amen.*

SECTION II.

The General Rules and Statutes of the Confraternity of the Rosary.

IT is (in the *first place*) to be presupposed, That there be a Priest or Dean of the *Rosary* impowred with sufficient authority from the Superiours of St *Dominicks* Order to receive such as desire to be admitted into this sacred Confraterdity : and to make choice of a Prefect, with such other Counselloùrs and Officers, as he shall conceive requisite for his assistance in order to the managing of the publick affairs of the Confraternity.

Secondly, That there be also a Chappel or Altar of the holy *Rosary* to which all the Brethren and Sisters have a particular Relation. *Pius Quintus* in his *Bull, Consueverunt*, and in his *Bull, Injunctum nobis*. Which being supposed, These are the general Rules with their explications.

The first Rule.

THat all faithful Christians (of whatsoever calling and condition) may
be received into this sacred Confraternity; without any obligation to pay
any thing for their entrance and admittance. *Leo the tenth Pastoris æterni* 1520.
pridie nonas Octob.

Annotations.

THe receiving of what is freely given,
and offered by devout persons; Either
for the ornaments of the Altar; or for the
entertainment of him that serves the Altar, or for the succouring of the poor Members of the Confraternity, is not hereby for-
bidden : But it is inhibited to exact any
thing as due, for any ones admittance.

First, Because it is a spiritual and holy
thing;

Secondly, To the end the Poor, as well
as the Rich, may enjoy this benefit;

Thirdly, Because this pious Institut,
intends not the Receivers advancement;
but his real good who is received.

The second Rule.

THere is to be a particular Book provided, wherein the Names and Sir-
names, of all such as are admitted, must
be enregistred.

Annotation.

IF the keeping of such a Register-Book,
or this manner of inrolling, be found in
some places and Countrey's inconvenient;
it abundantly suffices to have the Names
written and delivered to the Prefect of the
Confraternity, though they be presently
burnt and cancelled.

The third Rule.

VVHosoever is once thus admitted in any one place, is made
partaker of the prayers and merits of all
them that are of this Confraternity,
throughout the whole Universe.

Annotation.

AS concerning this large participation
of spiritual Benefits, See the tenth
Section in our larger Book of the Rosary.

The fourth Rule.

NOt only the living, but also the faithful departed (to wit the souls in Purgatory) may be received and inrolled in this Confraternity, and made partakers of these spiritual Benefits and Priviledges ; if any of the living Brethren and Sisters, (performing for their deceased friends, such pious duties and devotions as the Rules demand,) shall desire and procure it.

Annotation.

THis is grounded upon that Maxime, That all the Indulgences, which may be obtained by the living, are also applicable to the Dead.

The fifth Rule.

ALL the Brothers and Sisters are to recite once every week, the entire *Rosary*, or whole Psalter ; which they may (as themselves please) either perform together, or divide into three parts; for their greater ease and conveniency.

Annotation.

Annotation.

THe whole Pſalter or Roſary, is com-
poſed of 15. Paters, and 150 Aves:
The three parts contain each one five Paters, and fifty Aves. The Creed is commonly and commendably recited in the beginning, and added to the end of every third
part; with some other prayers, (as shall be
hereafter set down,) but are no necessary
part thereof.

The sixth Rule.

IN case of any lawful Impediment, the
Brothers and Sisters, causing the *Roſary* to be recited for them by another,
satisfy their own obligation.

Annotation.

THis is to be understood of some sufficiently excusing circumstance; for
'tis dangerous to trust a Procurator, when
we traffick for *Paradise.*

The seventh Rule.

IF through forgetfulness, multiplicity
of Employments, or negligence, (and
not out of contempt) they omit this

weekly Recital of the *Rosary*, It is no
sin, but only a privation (for that time)
of such spiritual benefits, whereof they
should otherwise have been partakers.

Annotation.

YEa, if *through carelefnefs and tepidi-
ty, any one fhall for a long time neglect
the faying of* the Rosary; *he ceafeth not
therefore to be a member of this Confraternity, but may return to his wonted devotions, and re-obtain the ufual graces and
benefits without any new admiffion.*

The eighth Rule.

ALL the *Rofa-ifts* shou'd be present at
the Mafs and Proceffion, which are
ufually performed in the Head-Chap-
pel, upon all the Feast daies of the sacred Virgin, and first Sundaies of the
months.

Annotation.

THis is enjoyned by Pius 4. in his
Brief Dum Præclara, &c. Both for
the gaining of fuch Plenary Indulgences
as are then, and there granted. And alfo,
that the devout Rofarifts, may honour
their facred Virgin-Mother with their

presence, and unitedly implore her Patronage and Protection.

The ninth Rule.

THe Dean, Prefect, and Officers of the Confraternity, are to cause four *Anniversaries*, to be every year celebrated at the Rosary Altar, for the Souls of their departed Brethren and Sisters, upon the morrows of our Blessed Ladies *four principal Festivities*; which, are her *Nativity, Annunciation, Purification, Assumption.* At which, all the *Rosarists* should also assist, that they may expect the same piety from their surviving Brethren for themselves after their own decease.

Annotation.

WHen the daies next following the four feasts before named, fall out to be either Sundaies, or some other greater solemnities: then these *Anniversary* duties are remitted to the next day, not so hindred.

An Advertisement.

SInce these two last Rules cannot well be practised in some places, The devout devotions, upon the daies before specified, at their private homes, and in their several habitations, with a Relation to such duties as are then solemnized in their Mother-Chappel; whereby they may gain the same spiritual benefits, as if they were personally there present: As is expresly granted by Pius Quinrus. Inter desiderabilia 28. June 1569. by Greg. 13. Cupientes: 24. Decemb. 1583. And by Sixtus Quintus. Dum ineffabilia meritorum: 30. Jan. 1586.

The tenth Rule.

THe great Feast of the Rosary, is not to be henceforth solemnized (as it was formerly,) upon the 25. day of March, but upon the first Sunday of October.

Annotation.

THis solemnity was thus translated (from the 25. of March to the first Sunday of October) by Pope Gregory the 13. who instituted the Feast of our blessed Lady, under the Title of the Rosary, as appears at large in his Brief beginning. Monet Apostolus, the first of April 1573. and ordained it should be (upon that first Sunday of October) perpetually celebrated in the Catholique Church; for an Eternal and graceful rememoration of that most remarkable and altogether miraculous Naval victory gained over the Turks, by a handful of Christians under the conduct of Don John of Austria, in the Bay of Lepanto in the Gulf of Achaia, upon the seventh day of October, which was then the first Sunday of that month in the year of our Redeemer 1571. about the end of Pius Quintus's Popedom, (who was the zealous promoter of this holy war) and at the beginning of the Popedom of his no less zealous Successor Gregory the thirteenth.

In which happy conflict, twenty of the Enemies Galleys were consumed with fire; as many more ingulphed by the waves; one hundred and fourscore taken, the great Bashaw with twenty five thousand Turkish Souldiers slain in the place, most of the residue brought away captives, twenty thousand Christians freed from their slavery, and the Catholique Cause asserted from most imminent danger and calamity.

And this glorious victory was obtained (as is piously conceived, saies this holy Pope Gregory in his Bull aforesaid) by the Prayers of the devout Rosarists, who even at that very time, were making their publick Processions in the several parts of

Christendom for this end, most earnestly imploring the divine assistance, (by the Intercession of their powerful Mother) that he would be pleased to protect his Church in her pressing necessity, and favour the just designs of those generous souls, who were then exposing their lives for the preservation of their Faith. Nor did the effect fail (but rather exceed) their hopes and expectation; as hath been briefly declared.

The eleventh Rule.

THe third Sunday of *April* is also to be solemnized by the devout *Rosarists*, according to the grant of Pope *Gregory* the 13. in his Bull, *cum sicut accepimus*, Jan. 3. 1579.

Annotation.

THe reason of the Institution of this Solemnity, was the signal Miracle which hapned in the City of Pavia; and which was briefly thus.

When in the year 1578. all Italy, and particularly Lumbardy, and more particularly the City Pavia, was afflicted with a violent Plague: The Inhabitants (by advice of the then and there Director of the Rosary) had recourse to the sacred

C   *Virgin*

Virgin-Mother in this their extream and urgent necessity; vowing to erect a Chappel, which should be dedicated *Virgini liberatrici*, after their deliverance from this eminent danger. The *Mother of Mercy* heard their prayers; obtained for them a present redress of their miseries, an entire cessation of the raging Pestilence; and they gratefully performed their promises, building a most sumptuous Chappel to her honour.

Seraphinus Siccus, *General of St Dominicks Order*, was an eye-witness of this famous *Miracle*. And Pope Gregory the 13. gave most ample and Plenary Indulgences to all such as should devoutly visit the *Chappel* aforesaid upon the third Sunday of April: which *Indulgences* were afterwards extended by the same Gregory 13. and Sixtus Quintus to all the other *Confraternities* of the sacred Rosary throughout the world.

SECTION III.

The Form of admitting Brothers and Sisters into this sacred Confraternity: With the blessing of their Beads, Roses, and Candles. And a Form of General Absolution at the hour of Death.

WHen the Dean of the *Rosary* hath maturely and prudently considered the quality and condition of the person who desires an admittance into this sacred Confraternity: [Which is a caution only necessary for such Countries and places where the Catholique Faith and Profession is under restraint, and where there may be danger of Persecution. For where our Religion is permitted to its full and free exercise, there needs no scruple be made of admitting any one to the *Rosary*, who humbly petitions for it, unless it be such a Person, whose life and conversation is notoriously and publickly scandalous, without hope of his being reclaimed from his wickednes.] He writes down his name, and enrolls him in the Register-book of the *Rosary*.

Which done, he causes the man or woman to kneel down, before the Altar of the *Rosary*, (if it be there present,) or some other devout Picture, or in any place whatsoever (as opportunity shall permit,) with a *Rosary-Candle* in his or her hand; and speaks to them briefly in this, or the like manner: Think with your selves (dear and devout Brethren and Sisters!) that you are now entring into a spacious and specious *Garden*, full

fraught with all forts of fpiritual fruits
and flowers : A *Garden*, wherein *finners*
may find food to convert them ; the
Good, means to better them ; the *Bad*,
motives to correct them ; the *Juft*,
waies to confirm them ; the *Tepid*, oc-
cafions to excite them ; the *Defolate*,
helps to comfort them ; the *Weak*, cor-
dialls to ftrengthen them ; the *Sick*,
Phyfick to cure them ; and all *Faithful*
Chriftians, fit conveniencies to fave
their fouls ; which is the end of our
Creation, the period of our pretenfions,
the Crown of all our laborious endeavours in this our earthly Pilgrimage.

Now thefe fruits are not only to be
gazed upon, and admired, but to be gathered, fwallowed, difgefted : Nor is it
fufficient to have your names enrolled
in the Rofary Catalogue, and to be ex-
ternally affociated to this facred Confraternity ; but you muft ferioufly re-
folve upon an honeft, honourable, holy
life and converfation ; a deteftation of
fin, vice, and vanity ; and in brief, a total reformation of your whole outward
and inward man. For fince you defire
to dedicate your felves this day particularly to Gods fervice, and to make a fpecial profeffion (of honouring his facred
Mother for the future, by becomming a

member of her Family; you muſt alſo
endeavour to ſurpaſs ſuch others, as pretend not to this height, holineſs, and
happineſs, in all ſorts of Chriſtian Piety, Vertue, and Perfection: That ſo really correſponding to what you out-
wardly promiſe, you may deſerve to obtain her deſired Patronge and Protection.

Say therefore with heart and mouth
as follows;

The Form of offering ones ſelf to the
Bleſſed Virgin.

THrice ſacred Virgin *Mary*, Mother
of God! I *N. N.* though moſt unworthy to be regiſtred amongſt your
ſervants, yet moved (by that Goodneſs
which the Angels admire in you) to an
ardent deſire of honouring, loving, and
ſerving you; do here this day with all
poſſible humility, ſincerity, and devotion, (in the preſence of my Angel Guardian, and the whole Court of Heaven)
make choice of you for my ſingular Lady, Advocate, and Mother; firmly pur-
poſing to honour, love, and ſerve you,
with all filial duty, diligence, and fidelity; and to procure (as much as it ſhall
lie in my power) that all others may do

I therefore most heartily beseech you, (O merciful and compassionate Mother!) by the precious Bloud which your dearly beloved Son, my blessed Saviour, shed for me in his bitter Passion; That you will be graciously pleased to receive and admit me into the number of your devout Clients, as one dedicated to your perpetual service.

Be you favourable to me (O Blessed Lady!) and obtain for me of your All-powerful Son, that I may so behave my self in all my Thoughts, Words, and Actions, as never more to think, speak, or act any thing displeasing to his sacred Majesty.

Grant furthermore (O my good and gracious Mother!) that I may never forget you, nor forfeit this my now made promise of honouring, loving, and serving you all the daies of my life; that so I may never be forgotten, forsaken, nor abandoned by you, but be alwaies protected, aided, and assisted by you, especiallie in the hour of my Death. Amen.

Then he receives him, or her into the Confraternity, by speaking these words, and giving them his Benediction, as follows.

BY the Authoritie, which is committed to me for this end, by the Superiours of the holy Order of St *Dominick:* I receive you into the Confraternitie of the *Rosary* of the most blessed Virgin *Mary:* And do admit you to a participation of all the spirituall Benefits, which (by the merits of Jesus Christ) the Brothers and Sisters of the sacred Rosarie do commonlie enjoy.

† *In the Name of the Father, and of the Son,* †, *and of the Holy Ghost. Amen.*

Then laying the Bedes upon the Altar; he puts a stole about his neck, and blesseth them for the use of the newlie received Brother or Sister: saying as followeth.

The Blessing of the Bedes of the Rosary.

Ver. *Adjutorium nostrum in nomine Domini.*

Resp. *Qui fecit cælum & terram.*

Psal. *Laudate Dominum in Sanctis ejus, laudate eum in firmamento virtutis ejus.*

Laudate eum in virtutibus ejus: laudate eum secundum multitudinem magnitudinem ejus.

Laudate eum in sono tubæ; laudate eum in psalterio & cithara.

Laudate eum in tympano, & choro: laudate eum in chordis & organo.

Laudate eum in cymbalis bene sonantibus; laudate eum in cymbalis jubilationis: omnis spiritus laudet Dominum.

Gloria Patri & Filio, &c.

Verf. *Dignare me laudare te virgo sacrata.*

Resp. *Da mihi virtutem contra hostes tuos.*

Verf. *Cum dederit dilectis suis somnum.*

Resp. *Ecce hæreditas Domini filii merces fructus ventris.*

Verf. *Domine exaudi orationem meam.*

Resp. *Et clamor meus ad te veniat.*

Verf. *Dominus vobiscum.*

Resp. *Et cum spiritu tuo.*

Oremus.

OMnipotens & misericors Deus, qui propter eximiam Charitatem tuam qua dilexisti nos, Filium tuum unigenitum Dominum nostrum Iesum Christum, pro Redemptione nostra, de cœlis in Terram descendere, & de Beatissima Virgine Maria Domina nostra utero, Angelo nunciante, carnem suscipere, crucemque ac mortem subire, & tertia die gloriose a morte resurgere voluisti, ut nos eriperes de potestate Diaboli: Obsecramus immensam clementiam tuam, ut hæc signa Rosarii, in

honorem & laudem ejusdem Genetricis
Filii tui, ab Ecclesia tua fideli dicata, Bene † dicas, & sancti † fices, eisque tantam
Sancti Spiritus infundas virtutem; ut
quicunque horam quodlibet secum porta-
verit, atque in domo sua reverenter tenuerit, & in eis ad te secundum ejusdem san-
Eta Confraternitatis Instituta, divina con-
templando mysteria devote oraverit; salu-
bri & perseverante devotione abunda; sit-
que consors & particeps omnium gratia-
rum, privilegiorum, & Indulgentiarum,
qua eidem Confraternitati per sacram Se-
dem Apostlicam concessa sunt; & ab omni
hoste visibili & invisibili semper & ubi-
que in hoc & in futuro saculo liberetur, &
in exitu suo, ab ipsa Beatissima Virgine
Maria Dei genitrice, tibi plenus bonis
operibus prasentari mereatur.

Per eundem Dominum nostrum Iesum
Christum Filium tuum, qui tecum vivit
& regnat, in unitate Spiritus Sancti Deus. Per omnia secula saculorum. Amen.

Then he besprinkles the Bedes with
holy-water; saying;

In nomine Patris, & Filii, & Spiritus
Sancti. Amen, and gives them to the
partie.

The blessing of the Roses for the use
of the Confraternitie.

Verf. *Adjutorium noftrum in nomine Domini.*

Refp. *Qui fecit cælum & terram.*

Pfalm. 132.

ECce quam bonum, & quam jucundum habitare fratres in unum.

Sicut unguentum in capite: quod defcendit in barbam, barbam Aaron.

Quod defcendit in oram veftimenti ejus: ficut ros Hermon, qui defcendit in montem Sion.

Quoniam illic mandavit Dominus benedictionem: & vitam ufque in faculum.

Gloria Patri & Filio, &c.

Antiphona.

Virgo Maria non eft tibi fimilis nata in mundo inter mulieres, florens ut rofa, fragrans ficut lilium.

Verf. *Ora pro nobis fancta Dei genitrix.*

Refp. *Ut digni efficiamur promiffionibus Chrifti.*

Verf. *Sicut dies verni circumdabant eam flores Rofarum.*

Refp. *Et lilia convallium.*

Oremus.

DEUS Creator & confervator generis humani, dator gratiæ fpiritualis, & largitor æternæ falutis! Benedictione tua facra bene † dicendum Rofas, quas *pro gratiis tibi exolvendis, cum devotione ac veneratione Beatæ semperque Virginis Mariæ hodie tibi præsentamus: & petimus benedici, & infundi eis per virtutem Sanctæ Crucis † benedictionem cælestem ut quiæs ad odoris suavitatem, & repellendas infirmitates humano usui tribuisti; talem signaculo sanctæ Cru † cis benedictionem accipiant, ut quibuscunque in infirmitatibus apposita fuerint, seu qui eas in domibus suis servaverint, vel cum devotione habuerint, aut portaverint, ab infirmitate sanentur, Discedant, contremiscant, & fugiant Diaboli cum suis ministris, de habitationibus illis; nec amplius tibi servientes inquietare præsumant. Per Christum Dominum nostrum. Amen.*

Then he sprinkles the Roses with holy Water, saying,

† *In nomine Patris, & Filii, & Spiritus Sancti. Amen.*

The Blessing of the Wax Candles for the Brothers and Sisters of the holy Rosary, to hold in their hands, at the hour of Death.

Verf. *Adjutorium nostrum in nomine Domini.*

Resp. *Qui fecit cælum & terram.*

Canticum.

Nunc dimittis servum tuum Domine: secundum verbum tuum in pace.

Quia viderunt oculi mei: salutare tuum.

Quod parasti: ante faciem omnium populorum :

Lumen ad revelationem gentium: & gloriam plebis tuæ Israel.

Gloria Patri &c.

Antiphona.

AVE Regina Cœlorum,
Ave Domina Angelorum.
Salve Radix, Salve Porta.
Ex qua mundo lux est orta,
Gaude virgo gloriosa,
Super omnes speciosa,
Vale O valde decora,
Et pro nobis Christum exora.

Vers. Post partum virgo inviolata permansisti.

Resp. Dei Genitrix intercede pro nobis.

Vers. Domine exaudi orationem meam.
Resp. Et clamor meus ad te veniat.
Vers. Dominus vobiscum.
Resp. Et cum Spiritu tuo.

Oremus.

DOmine Iesu Christe, lux vera, qui illuminas omnem hominem, veni-

entem in hunc mundum! Effunde per intercessionem Virginis Mariæ matris tuæ, & per quindecem ejus Rosarii mysteria, Bene † dictionem tuam super hos cereos & candelas, & sanctifica eas lumine tuæ gratiæ, & concede propitius ut sicut hæc luminaria igne visibili accensa, nocturnas depellunt tenebras; Ita corda nostra invisibili igne, id est, Spiritus Sancti Splendore illustrata, omnium vitiorum cæcitate careant, ut puro mentis oculo cernere semper possimus, quæ tibi sunt placita, & nostræ saluti utilia: quatenus post hujus sæculi caliginosa discrimina, ad lucem indeficientem pervenire mereamur. Qui vivis & regnas Deus, in secula seculorum. Amen.

Oremus.

Domine Iesu Christe, splendor gloriæ, & figura substantiæ Patris, & virginalis uteri fructus! Qui per temporalem Nativitatem tuam divinæ Filiationis imaginem per gratiam hominibus contulisti, illosque fratres vocare dignatus es: Auge in nobis famulis tuis, (in Confraternitate virginis Matris tuæ gloriantibus) Spiritum gratiæ quem dedisti, & has candelas quas in honorem Nominis ejus suscipimus, ita Bene † dicere & sancti † ficare digneris, ut quicunque eas in manibus accensas tenuerit, ab omnibus libere-

*tuis tentationibus, & in hora mortis suæ,
remissionem omnium peccatorum percipi-
at; & demum ad Te, qui verum lumen
es, ipsa dirigente perveniat. Qui vivis &
regnas in sæcula sæculorum. Amen.*

Then he sprinkles the Candles with
holy Water, saying, *In nomine,&c.*

The General Absolution, or, Plenary Indulgence to be applied to the Brethren and Sisters of the Rosary, at the hour of their Death.

The sick Person (or some other for
him) having said the *Confiteor*, the
Priest standing up, saies.

*Misereatur tui omnipotens Deus, & di-
missis peccatis tuis, perducat te ad vitam
æternam.*

*Indulgentiam absolutionem & Remis-
sionem peccatorum tuorum tribuat tibi
omnipotens & misericors Dominus.*

Then holding his right hand over his
head : he proceeds.

*Dominus noster Jesus Christus Filius
Dei vivi, qui Beato Petro Apostolo
suo dedit potestatem ligandi atque solven-*

di ; per pi ssimam suam misericordiam te
absolvat ; Et authoritate ipsius & Beato-
rum Apostolorum ejus Petri & Pauli, &
authoritate Apostolica, Absolvo te a vinculo Excommunicationis majoris & mi-
noris, [suspensionis & interdicti] in quantum possum, & tu indiges; & Restituo te
Sacramentis Ecclesia, Communioni &
unitati fidelium. † In nomine Pa † tris,
& Fi † lii, & Spiritus † Sancti. Amen.

Item, Apostolica authoritate mihi
commissa & tibi concessa, Absolvo te ab
omnibus peccatis tuis, quocumque toto de-
cursu vita tua quomodocumque commi-
sisti, de quibus corde contritus, & ore con-
fessus es, & quorum memoriam non habes,
nec recordaris usque in praesentem diem, &
de quibus confiteri minus è recordatus
fuisti, Et Restituo te illi Innocentiae, in qua
eras quando Baptizatus fuisti, ac puritati
eidem, in quantum claves sancta Matris
Ecclesiae se extendunt. Et per Indulgentiam plenariam a summis Pontificibus; In-
nocentio octavo & Pio quinto, confratri-
bus Sanctissimi Rosarii in articulo mortis
constitutis concesserunt, liberet te Misericor-
dissimus Deus a praesentis & futura vita
poenis ; dignetur Purgatorii cruciamenta re-
mittere, portas Inferni claudere, Paradisi
januam aperire, teque ad gaudia sempiterna per sacratissima sua vita, passionis &

glorificationis Mysteria sanctissimo Rosa-
rio comprehensa perducere. Et hoc; si de
qua agrota Infirmitate decedas; si non,
ex misericordia Dei, salva sit tibi, plena-
ria hac Indulgentia donec fueris in mortis
articulo constitutus. In nomine Patris, &
Filii, & Spiritus † Sancti. Amen.

Another shorter form of General Absolution out of Antoninus. *part. 1.*
tit. 10. cap. 3. sect. 5.

Authoritate Apostolica, mihi pro nunc
commissa, concedo tibi plenam omni-
um peccatorum tuorum Indulgentiam &
Remissionem. In Nomine Patris, &
Fi † lii & Spiritus † Sancti. Amen.

SECTION IV.

Of the pious use of Processions.

WHereby the devout *Rosarists*
Religiously honour God, and
the sacred Virgin *Mary,* upon the first
Sundaies of the months, and upon the
seven feasts of our blessed Lady; to
wit, The *purification, Annunciation, Vi-*
sitation, Assumption, Nativity, Presen-
tation, and *Conception,* and upon the

Saturdaies, and other Festival daies of the fifteen Mysteries.

1. The word Procession signifies *literally* a passing forward from one place to another : *Allegorically,* a progress from vertue to vertue : *Tropologically,* our Peregrination upon earth : *Anagogically,* our tendencie towards heaven.

2, *Processions* had their beginning in the Age of the old Patriarcks ; in which the Ark of the Testament was reverently *carried* to and fro by the *Priests* of the Tribe of *Levi,* who were peculiarly set apart, for that *sacred purpose,* and performed that office, with great *pompe* and solemnitie : As also when *David* brought the Ark into the Tabernacle, and *Solomon* into the Temple, with Hymns, Canticles, and all sorts of musical instruments, and placed it under the wings of the there prepared Cherubins.

3. Our solemn Processions, seem in all things to imitate the Egression of the Israelites out of Egypt. For [1] That people was freed by *Moses,* out of the hands of *Pharao* : We, by *Christ,* out of the Clutches of the Devil. [2] *Ensigns* were carried before their Troops : And before us *Crosses* and *Banners.* [3.] A pillar of *Fire* went before them : Burning *Candles* are born before us. [4.] There

the *Levites* carryed the Tabernacle of
the Covenant, and the Ark of the Te-
ftament : Here, the *Priefts* carry the
Statua's of Saints, the Reliques of the
Martyrs, or the Pix with the facred Eu-
charift. [5.] *Aaron* the *High Prieft*
follow'd them in his Pontificall habits ;
and our *Chief Prieft* follows us in his
Cope, and Church Ornaments. [6.]
There was *Mofes* with his Rod : Here is
(a *Prelate*, with his Crofier) a Prefect
with his Official ftaffe [7.] The people
there march'd in compleat *armour* ; the
Clergie-men are here covered with facred *veftments*. [8.] They were be-
fprinkled with *Bloud*: we with holy
water. [9.] They had a *Jefus* for their
conductor, and conquerour, we have a
Jefus. [10.] They came at laft into the
Land of *Promife* : and we come up to the
holy *Altar*, in hope to arrive one day at
Heaven, our promifed home, and happy
Countrey.

    4. Our Proceffions are the *Memorials*
of our Redeemers mercies, minding us
of the Proceffions *he* made from his
eternal Fathers bofom, into the womb
of the bleffed Virgin, from her womb
into the Manger: from the Manger, to
Jerufalem : from *Jerufalem*, to the
Mount *Olivet* : from Mount *Olivet*,

back to his heavenly Father; All which
we gratefully commemorating, move
after his sacred Standard the Cross, and
make to him our humble supplications,
that we may pass after him, from this
our Pilgrimage, to his Paradise: from
the Church Militant, to the Triumphant.

5. Our Processions (especially those
of the pious *Rosarists*) are also *Comme-
morations*, and *Imitations* of the blessed
Virgin-Mothers journeys upon Earth:
when she [1.] carried, or [2.] accompanied, or [3.] followed her beloved
Son Jesus; [1.] when she carried him
in her sacred womb into the Mountains,
to the house of *Zachary* and *Elizabeth*,
and into the *Bethleem* stable: and when
she carried him in her sacred arms into
the Temple, and into *Egypt*; [2.] when
she accompanied him, being twelve years
old to *Jerusalem*: and being thirty years
old throughout *Judea* and *Galile* in his
preachings. [3.] when she followed him
laden with his Cross to Mount *Calvary*.

And surely, if all the journeys and
pilgrimages from place to place, of Jesus and *Mary* upon Earth, may not properly be called Processions: yet they
may fitly be styled the exemplary Pattern of our Processions, which are made
to their likeness, and in their memory

6. There are four chief and solemn Processions celebrated yearly and universally by the Catholique Church. [1.] in the purification of the blessed Virgin *Mary*; [2.] upon Palm-Sunday: [3.] upon Easter day: [4.] upon Ascension day, in memorie and representation of that last Procession, wherein the Disciples waited upon our Redeemer to Mount *Olivet*, to see him assumpted into Heaven: where it is to be noted, that in the Primitive Church, there were made two weekly Processions: one upon *Sunday*, in memory of the Resurrection; and another upon *Thursday*, in memory of the Ascention: Whence sprung up that common Proverb of Thursdaies being near a kin to Sunday. But when afterwards the Festivities of Saints became multiplied, the Solemnity and Procession of Thursday was abrogated by *Pope Agapitus*, and transferr'd also to that of Sunday: which is therefore still observed in the joynt memorie of the Resurrection and Ascention, in all Cathedral and conventual Churches.

7. To these four Processions may be added those of the *greater* and *less Litanies*; which are also yearly and generally celebrated; the Procession of the *great Litanies*, upon St. *Marks* day,

instituted by Pope *Gregory* the Great, to implore the divine assistance against the then raging Pestilence ; the Procession of the *less Litanies*, upon the three dayes before the Ascension begun by St. *Mamertus* Bishop of *Vienna*, to implore a remedy against the many miseries, wherewith *France* was then afflicted.

Both which customs were afterwards confirmed by the Church, and commanded to be kept by all her faithful children.

8. Having prefated thus much of *Processions* in *general*, let us briefly consider them of the sacred *Rosary in particular*, which (as aforesaid) are made upon each first Sunday of the month, and the blessed Virgins Festivities.

1. The first Ceremonie in these (as in all other) Processions is the *carriage of the Cross*, [1.] because it is the ancient and perpetual custom of the Catholique Church, to carry the *Cross* before in all her supplications. [2.] because the *Cross* is the common sign, mark, and cognisance of all Christians. [3.] to shew that

Cross : is again foyled, defeated, and put to flight by these Proceffions.

2. The fecond is, *the reliques of Saints*. [1.] to profefs the Communion of the Saints of both Churches, Triumphant and Militant. [2.] to declare that we beg the Saints interceffions. [3.] to honour God in them.

3. The third is, the *Statua of the bleffed Virgin*. [1.] this is the cuftome of the Church, and the tradition of our Ancestors. [2.] it is a confufion to Heretiques, and Image-haters, and a motive to us (at the fight of her facred Reprefentative) to pray unto *her* for their converfion, *who is entitled by the Church, the confoundrefs of all Herefies throughout the whole World* ; (This praying for the converfion of Heretiques, being one of the principal caufes of thefe our Proceffions.) [3.] it is a practice, which Heaven hath frequently approved of, by many fignal miracles.

Let us infift a little upon this point, and prove this carriage of our bleffed Ladies Image or Statua in Proceffions to

fute, not only such flat Heretiques, as
fondly affirm these manner of Procession-
ons to be no other than modern and
monkish inventions: but also such ignorant and critical Catholiques, as scruple
to render this sort of honour to *her*,
who can never be sufficiently honoured
by any humane industry.

Poor deceived, and undevout wretches,
deserving rather to be pitied for your
ignorance, than to be satisfied by argu-
ments, in a subject of so clear evidence!
we will stick stedfastly to our well-taken
up Tenents, continue cheerfully in our
rightly intended devotions, and pray
perseverantly for your illumination, in
our sacred Processions, hoping at last
to conquer your peevishness by our piety and charity, and by her power and
intercession: in whose name, for whose
love, and to whose honour, we (the
children of *Mary*)are gathered together
(as brethren in one heart, soul and mind)
to march under the Banner of the sacred Rosary.

We therefore (returning to our intended purpose) confidently affirm, that
the *Examples* of our pious Ancestors,
and the *miracles* wrought by the carriage of our blessed Mothers Images in
Procession, are sufficient warrants and

motives to induce us to the same devout
practice; *Examples* and *miracles*; which
may abundantly be read throughout
the whole body of the Ecclesiastical hi-
stories; from whence we will borrow
these few following instances.

And to begin with our great St. *Gregory* (who sate in the Roman chair, in
the year of Christ, 601. at which time
the Inhabitants of that City dyed suddenly, lying in their beds, sitting in their
houses, walking in the fields, standing in
the streets: so violently raging was the
pestilential contagion!) he indicting a
three daies supplication, *let us* (saies he)
*O my afflicted children! meet together in
the Church of blessed Mary, the perpetual
Virgin, and holy Mother of our Lord Jesus Christ, and there with sighs, tears, and
prayers implore the divine mercy, for the
remission of our sins, and the remedie of
our miseries.*

The people being gathered together
accordingly, *He* in his own person, takes
the sacred Virgins Picture, drawn by
St. *Lukes* pensil, (which Picture is carefully kept, and highly honoured even till
this day, in the same Church of St. *Marie ad Prasepe*, or, *of the manger* in a sumptuous chappel, built by *Paulus Quintus*,
for that purpose) and carries it along

the street in Procession; when behold
the celestial Spirits, are heard ecchoing
forth the blessed Virgins praises, in answer to their pious hymns and Litanies,
the air is fil.ed with the melodious har-
monie of angelical Choristers, in toning
sweet Anthems to her honour, and saluting her with these sacred words,
(used ever since by the Church in the
Paschal Office.)

Regina cœli lætare, &c. O Queen of
Heaven rejoyce, Alleluja, for he whom
you deserved to bear, Alleluja. Is risen
from death as he fortold, Alleluja. To
which the holy Pope, by divine inspiration, added of his own.

Pray unto God for us, Alleluia, and
an Angel is seen upon the top of the
Adrian Tower, putting up a Sword into
its scabbard.

The astonished St. *Gregory,* inferring
from that action, a mitigation of the
divine indignation denounces to the no
less ravished people, a *Quietus est,* from
the Court of Heaven.

And (O admirable prodigy of the
divine mercy! O clear testimony of
holy *Maries* Power!) there immediat-
ly followed a full and happy delivery
from that dire disease and mortality.

And is not this only miracle, (wrought
in

in the open view of the world, done in the head-Citie of the Universe, acted (as to that part of it which is cavilled at,) by the Churches chief Pastor, and Christs Vicegerent upon earth, and registred by so many undeniable and authentick Authors) able to *confound you*: O Heretiques and Image-haters! capable to *convert* you: O half-Catholiques, and dishonourers of holy *Mary*! sufficient to *comfort* you, O devout children of the sacred Rosary! yet cast an eye upon some others of like nature, in the succeding Ages.

St. *Stephen* the third, making a Procession on his bare feet, together with the Roman Clergie and people, and carrying a holy Image on his own shoulders to the same Church of St. *Mary at the Manger*, implored and obtained the like heavenly assistance.

Sergius the Patriarch of *Constantinople*, carried the sacred Virgins Image in procession about the City-wall, and received a present and miraculous remedy against *Caganus*, and the rest of the Scithians, his besieging enemies.

The same was done under *Heraclius* the Emperour in his Persian expedition: who thereupon obtained a compleat victory over his enemies, destroying

(with the loss only of fifty of his own
Souldiers) the two vast Armies of Duke
Razates, whose golden Armour he afterwards hung up as a trophe to the victo-
rious Virgin.

And when the same City of *Constantinople* was again straightned by the cruel *Saracens*, the distressed Inhabitants
making their accustomed addresses to
their powerful Patroness, and carrying
her sacred *Effigies*, as formerly about
their besieged walls, saw their Enemies
suddenly perishing before their faces;
some with fire from heaven, the rest
with famine, pestilence, shipwrack, and
such like severe punishments: In memory of which miraculous delivery the
grateful Citizens celebrated an annual
Festivity in *her* honour, by *whose* help
they obtained it.

Many more examples might be here
multiplied: in *Constantine* the last Ea-
stern Emperour, *Emmanuel* the Conquerour of *Pannonia*, *Joannes Ximisca*
the Overcomer of the Russians, *Joannes
Commenius* the Triumpher over the
Persians, &c. But these few are more
than sufficient to vindicate this our
pious custome, not only from Innovati-
on, but from all other aspersions whatsoever.

The fourth Ceremonie in these our Processions is the carriage of *wax Candles*, or *Torches*, in imitation of the Churches ancient custome, observed upon the day of the blessed Virgins Purification: of which our St. *Bede* said long since: *This good custom spreading it self abroad, was kept also in the other Festivities of the sacred Mother, and Virgin Mary.*

The fifth and last Ceremonie is the singing or reciting of the Litanies of our blessed Lady of the *Rosary:* which Litanies are sung in the Church called our Lady of *Minerva* in *Rome,* and in many other Churches throughout all *Italy* upon every Saturday, by the approbation and authority of Pope *Gregory* the thirteenth in his Brief bearing date, *April* the fifteenth 1580. which Litanies are as follows after this Elevation.

An Elevation for the Procession of the Rosary.

O Sacred Virgin-Mother! Conduct my foot-steps, my thoughts, and my prayers; [1.] That I may honour your Excellencies, Greatnesses and Glories, [2.] That I may submit to the So-

veraign power you have over me ; [3.]
That I may implore and obtain your favour and mercy, which are the three
Ends and Intentions I propose to my
self in accompanying this sacred Procession, which is now made in your
honour by your faithful children and
servants.

I intend also hereby to honour all
your sacred courses and journeys.

The *first*, (which in your tender age)
you made to the Temple, to present and
consecrate your self entirely to the divine Majesty, dedicating to him your
body by a vow of perpetual Virginity ;
your soul, by a resolution of future affection; and all your Actions, by a Sacrifice of your whole life to his service.

The *second*, which (being declared
Gods Mother) you made into the
Mountains, to visite your Cousin *Elizabeth*, to sanctifie St. *John Baptist*, to bless
that whole Family.

The *third*, which (being big with the
divine Word Incarnate)you made from
Nazareth to *Bethleem*, to shew your
loyal Obedience to an Earthly Princes
Edict : but more, to profess your
prompt subjection to the Heavenly
Kings Providence.

The

The *fourth*, which (bearing your bleſſed Babe in your arms) you made from *Bethleem* to the Temple, to offer up to the Eternal Father, the higheſt and holleſt Oblation that ever was, or ſhall be offered to his divine Majeſty: An *Offering*, which was the full accompliſhment of all the ancient Figures and Sacrifices.

The *fifth*, which, (to avoid *Herods* cruelty) you made with your tender Son *Jeſus*, and your dear Husband St. *Joſeph* into *Egypt*.

The *ſixth*, which (having loſt your beloved *Jeſus*) you made to *Jeruſalem*, carefully ſeeking him.

The *ſeventh*, which (during his three laſt years preaching; you made throughout *Judea*, and *Paleſtine* ; painfully following him.

The *eighth*, which (in the time of his Paſſion,) you made to Mount *Calvary* dolefully accompanying him.

The *ninth*, which (having compleated your happy Pilgrimage upon earth) you made to Paradiſe, to remain there, the glorious Empreſs of Heaven for evermore.

In the Honour of theſe your journeys, O ſacred Virgin! (Star of the Sea, and Guide of my life) I will take my steps in this present Procession; humbly desiring to run after the odours of your sweet perfumes, (that is, to imitate the examples of your heroick vertues) that so I may be found worthy to accompany you in Celestial glory, and there with you to bless, praise and honour, the Father, Son, and Holy Ghost for all Eternity, *Amen.*

SECTION V.

The Litanies of our Blessed Lady of the Rosary.

Antiphona. *Sub tuum Præsidium confugimus Sancta Dei Genitrix, nostras deprecationes ne despicias in necessitatibus nostris, sed a periculis cunctis libera nos semper, Virgo gloriosa & benedicta, Domina nostra, Mediatrix nostra, Advocata nostra, tuo filio nos reconcilia, tuo Filio nos commenda, tuo Filio nos repræsenta, nunc, & in hora mortis nostræ.*

Kyrie Eleyson.
Christe Eleyson.
Kyrie Eleyson.
Sancta Trinitas unus Deus,

Virgo, Audi nos.
Virgo, Exaudi nos.
Sancta Maria,
Sancta Dei Genitrix,
Sancta Virgo Virginum,
Mater Pietatis,
Mater Veritatis,
Mater Charitatis,
Virgo Potentissima,
Virgo Prudentissima,
Virgo Clementissima,
Ancilla Domini mitis,
Ancilla Christi humilis,
Ancilla Dei fidelis,
Sponsa æterni Patris,
Filia summi Regis,
Templum Spiritus sancti,
Domus Dei,
Sanctuarium Christi,
Sacrarium Paracleti,
Speculum Justitiæ,
Sedes Sapientiæ,
Fons Misericordiæ,
Salus Infirmorum,
Refugium Miserorum,
Advocata Peccatorum,
Stella rutilantior,
Luna pulchrior,
Sole splendidior,
Scala Cœli,
Porta Paradisi,

Ora pro nobis.

Domina Mundi,
Cedrus Fragrans,
Myrrha Conservans,
Balsamum Distillans,
Flos Virginitatis,
Lilium Castitatis,
Rosa Puritatis,
Palma Virens,
Virga Florens,
Gemma Refulgens,
Oliva speciosa,
Columba Formosa,
Mulier Gratiosa,
Rubus Incombustus,
Hortus Conclusus,
Puteus Signatus,
Vellus Gedeonis,
Favus Sampsonis,
Thronus Salomonis,
Vitis fructificans,
Navis abundans,
Arca Salvans,
Gloria Saeculi,
Honor Populi,
Nutrix Parvuli,
Regina Angelorum,
Regina Patriarcharum,
Regina Prophetarum,
Regina Apostolorum,
Regina Martyrum,
Regina Confessorum,

Regina Prædicatorum,
Regina Virginum,
Regina Sanctorum Omnium,
Regina Sanctissimi Rosarii,

} Ora pro nobis.

Ab omni malo & Peccato,
   Libera nos Domina.
Per salutiferam Nativitatem & beatam
Præsentationem tuam,
   Libera nos Domina.
Per sanctam Purificationem & cælestem
vitam tuam,
   Libera nos Domina.
Per admirabilem Assumptionem, & glo-
riosam Coronationem tuam,
   Libera nos Domina.
Ut veram pænitentiam & perseveranti-
am, nobis impetrare digneris,
   Te rogamus Domina.
Ut Ecclesiasticos ordines & Catholicos
Principes conservare digneris,
   Te rogamus Domina.
Ut hanc nostram, Cunctasque Congre-
gationes tibi devotas augere & Conser-
vare digneris,
   Te rogamus Domina.
Ut hanc nostram, Cunctasque Congre-
gationes tibi devotas, augere, & con-
servare digneris,
   Te Rogamus Domina.
Ut Populo Christiano Pacem, salutem,
& abundantiam obtinere digneris,

Ut Navigantibus portum, pro Fide pug-
nantibus Victoriam, Fidelibus vitam,
defunctis Requiem æternam Impetrare
digneris,

Te rogamus Domina.

Vers. Ave de cœlis Alma,

Resp. Succurre nobis Domina.

Vers. Ave de cœlis Pia,

Resp. Fer opem nobis Domina.

Vers. Ave de cœlis Dulcis,

Resp. Intercede pro nobis Domina.

Vers. Sancta Maria, Mater Christi,

Resp. Audi rogantes servulos; & im-
petratam nobis cœlitus tu defer Indulgentiam.

Vers. Orate pro nobis omnes Sancti
Dei,

Resp. Ut digni efficiamur promissionibus Christi.

Vers. Salvos fac servos tuos, & Ancil-
las tuas.

Resp. Deus meus, sperantes in te.

Oremus.

Supplicationem servorum tuorum, Deus miserator exaudi, ut qui in Societa-
te sanctissimi Rosarii Dei genitricis &
Virginis Mariæ congregamur, ejus inter-
cessionibus a te, de instantibus periculis
eruamur.

E 2   Deus

Deus, cujus unigenitus, per vitam, mortem, & Resurrectionem in nostræ carnis substantia, nobis salutis æterna præmia comparavit, Da famulis tuis hæc omnia per sanctum Rosarium recensentibus, imitari quod gessit, sentire qua pertulit, & assequi quod promisit.

Tribue, quæsumus Domine, omnes Angelos & Sanctos tuos jugiter pro nobis orare, & eos clementer exaudire digneris.

Ecclesiæ tuæ, Domine, preces placatus admitte, ut destructis adversitatibus, & erroribus universis, secura tibi servias libertate.

Custodi (Domine !) famulum tuum, N. Patronum nostrum, pro quo Majestati tuæ supplicamus, ut Benedictionis tuæ Virtute in Viis omnibus dirigatur, & contra omnes hostium, tam visibilium quam invisibilium, insidias defendatur ; Per Christum Dominum nostrum.

Versic. *Ave Maria,*

Resp. *Gratia plena,*

Versic. *Dominus tecum.*

Resp. *Benedicta tu in mulieribus, &* Benedictus fructus ventris tui, Iesus, Iesus Christus Amen.

Versic. *Sancta Maria, Mater Dei, ora* pro nobis Peccatoribus, nunc & in hora mortis nostræ.

Resp. *Et fidelibus defunctis requiem sem-*

Benedictio.

Nos cum Prole pia Benedicat Virgo †
Maria.

A devout recommendation to the ever
blessed Virgin, after Procession.

O Mother of Mercy, Mother of Power, Mother of *Jesu,* Mother and
Advocate of poor and repentant Sinners, to whom your care and affection
is greater than that of a Mother to her
child! Into your sacred hands, and
heart, I do most humbly recommend
this day and for ever my body and soul,
all that I am and have, my life and my
death, that in all I may seek your Sons
honour, and find my own happiness.

Beg for me (O blessed Mother!) diligence to seek *Jesu,* love to find him,
obedience to follow him, purity to see
him, charity to embrace him, patience
to suffer for him, devotion to sigh after
him, indifferencie to adhere to him, and
perseverance to remain with him for
evermore.

O Empress of Heaven, Beauty of Angels, and Lady of Love! How long shall
nature, sensuality, and selfishness bear

sway? How long shall I seek, and not find; sigh, and not enjoy; live, and not truly love *Jesus* and *Mary*, the good Son, and glorious Mother, the holy Fruit, and happy Tree.

O my compassionate Mother! obtain for me your poor child, counsel in all my doubts, comfort in all my distresses, courage in all my temptations, and confidence in all my troubles.

Help me (O holy Mother of my Lord Jesus!) to be truly humble in my self, truly devout and loyal to my God, truly obedient to my Superiours, and truly meek to all.

Be you alwaies mindful of me (O my dear Mother!) both living and dying; and then especially have a care of me, when I forget my self by falling into Sin, and when my Soul must be forced out of my Body by death; that after death I may see, praise, and love both you and your Son *Jesus* for all eternity, *Amen.*

SECTION VI.

*An Explication of the material parts of
the Rosary, which are 1. The Sign of
the Cross. 2. The Creed. 3. The Lords
Prayer. 4. The Angelical Salutation.*

THE *Rosary,* is begun and ended with
the *Sign of the Cross,* and saying of
the *Creed;* and consists in the frequent
Repetition of the *Lords Prayer,* and
Angelical Salutation; and in the continual *Meditation* upon the chief Mysteries of our Redeemer and his sacred
Mother : therefore you are, devout Rosarists ! first to ground your selves in the
knowledge and understanding (at least
in some measure) of these Prayers, and
of these Mysteries ; that so your devotions may prove more efficacious, and
your Prayers be performed with more
gust and satisfaction.

To which end you may profitably
read over and peruse this ensuing explication of them : and (as often as your
occasions shall permit, and your devotion serve) recite them, as they are
hereafter affectively enlarged and para-

Of the Sign of the Cross, wherewith we begin our Rosary.

THe sign of the *Cross*, was prefigured and announced by the *Prophets*, taught and recommended by our Redeemer *Christ Jesus*: and ever used and practised in the *Catholique Church*.

With this *sign* all faithful Christians ought to begin all their actions (according to that Counsel and command of St. *Cyprian*; Make this *sign* both eating and drinking; and sitting and standing; and speaking and walking: And of St. *Hierome*. At every action, and upon all occasions, let the hand imprint a *Cross*:) But much more careful should they be, to begin their prayers and devotions, (which are the chief Acts of Religion) with this sacred *sign*; And most of all, ought they so to begin the recital of their *Rosary*, which is the most eminent sort of prayer and devotion.

St. *Augustine*, alleadges several Reasons for this general custome of all Christians: Because this *sign* of the *Cross* (laies he) directs the course of our Pilgrimage, instructs us for our combate, helps us in our conflict, strengthens us for our Conquest; . It destroys all dangers, and defends us from all Diabolical subtilties and machinations. To which may be added,

1. That this sign of the *Cross*, is a compendious Profession of the Christian Faith, wherein the Mystery of the sacred Trinity, the Incarnation, and Passion of our Blessed Saviour, and the Remission of sins by his merits is briefly taught and declared.

2. It is a certain badge, by which Orthodox Christians are known and distinguished from *Sectaries* and Infidels: we are all said to be Christians, (saies *St. Augustin*) for we are all signed with Christs signet.

3. It is an Invocation of the divine assistance in all our actions, for by this *sign* we invoke the sacred Trinity to our ayd by the mediation of our Saviours Passion.

4. It affords us spiritual comfort and courage; For if thou art not ashamed (saies *St. Augustine*) to make this sign exteriourly before men; thou mayest confidently expect to feel the divine sweetness in thy soul.

5. It is a Meditation, and Imitation of our Redeemers Passion. When thou

Goest

signest thy self with the *Cross*, (saies *St. Chrysostome*.) ruminate in thy mind the whole cause of the *Cross*, and thou shalt easily quench the fires of all thy passions.

6. It gives us hopes of our salvation. For what may not *he* hope, *who* beholds Christ dying on the Cross for his Redemption ; and *who* looks upon Christ more faithfully, than *he*, who frequently imprints his *Cross* upon his heart and forehead? To which the Apostle alluding exhorts all Christians to remember, at *how dear a rate they are bought*, and to glorifie and carry God in their Bodies.

7. It inflames our souls in the divine love and charity. For who can consider Christ expiring on the *Cross* for his sake, and continue cold and tepid? God commends his love towards us, (saies the Apostle,) *In that while we were yet sinners, Christ died for us.*

8 It averts from us Gods indignation and revenge: In which sense, that saying of the *Psalmist* is understood by *St. Gregory of Nice*, and by *St. Hierom*, *Thou* (O Lord!) *hast given a sign to them that fear thee, that they may fly from before the Bow.*

9. It defends us from all our enemies: ·

ſo the ſame Fathers explicate that other paſſage of the Pſalmiſt ; ſhew ſome *ſign* upon me for good, that they who hate me, may ſee it, and be aſhamed, becauſe thou (O Lord) haſt holpen me, and comforted me.

10. It drives away the Devils. Sign thy ſelf (ſaies St. *Cyrl*) with the *Croſs* in the forehead ; that the Devil perceiving the Kings character, may be affrighted and fly from thee : And again, This *ſign* (ſaies he) is a comfort to Chriſtians, and a terrour to the Devils : And the Martyr *Ignatius* : The ſign of the *Croſs* is a Trophe againſt the power of the Prince of this world, which hearing and beholding, he fears and trembles.

Finally, The ſign of the *Croſs* (ſaies St. *Cyril*) is the *Seminary* of all vertues : and in it alone (ſaies S. *Ambroſe*) conſiſts the proſperity of all Chriſtians.

And if any ſhall queſtion you (O Chriſtians ! ſaies *Tertullan*) whence this Ceremony had its firſt riſe and origin ? Anſwer them boldly : Tradition hath taught it, cuſtome hath confirmed it, Faith hath practiſed it.

Since therefore this *ſign* is of ſo great power and efficacy, againſt the Devils ;

of dangers; so undrainable a fountain of all desirable good and happines (as in these few words supported by the authority of such ancient and learned Fathers, seems sufficiently declared:) Let us (O devout Fellow-members of the sacred *Rosary!*) be carefull to arm our selves therewith, upon all occasions, at all times, in all places (and especially at the beginning and end of our *Psalter*,) remembring that we are spiritual Souldiers, listed by Christ our Captain, to fight under the banner of his blessed *Cross*, against the World, the Flesh and the Devil; and undoubtedly hoping by vertue thereof, to overcome and vanquish them.

Of the Apostles Creed, which is, The first part of the Rosary.

THe Apostolical *Symbol*, or *Creed*; is so called; for that it was made and compiled (saith *St. Clement*) by the twelve Apostles, being yet together, each one of them adding what was conceived necessary; to the end, that when they were separated, they might preach this Rule of Faith to all Nations: (which as *St. Augustine* largely declares) is a plain, short, Compleat comprehension of our Faith, that so its *Plainness* might correspond to the Hearers capacity; its *Shortness* to their memorie, its *Compliantness* to the contained doctrine. For that which in Greek is named *Symbolum*, is called Collation in Latine because the Catholique Doctrine is compendiously knit and collected together in this divine *Symbol*; which signifies also *Indicium*, a mark, note, or token, whereby Orthodox Believers might be known and distinguished from all others. Now some of the Reasons, why this sacred *Creed* ought to be recited at the entrance upon our *Rosary*, may be briefly these.

1. Because Order and Reason seem to require, that after the solemn confession and Invocation of the Holy Trinity, (which is done, (*as aforesaid*) by making the sign of the *Cross*:) We should in the next place, make a profession of what we believe of the Trinity.

2. Because *Faith*, being the Foundation of Prayer; (as the Apostle expresly tells us; *He that comes to God, must believe*) We do hereby most fitly at the beginning of our *Prayer* renew, excite, and reduce our *Faith* from its habit, to an act.

3. Because the Church begins and ends the Canonical Office with a *Creed*, and

and the *Rosary* (as *hath been declared*)
is an Imitation of the Davidical Psalter
and Church Psalmodie.

4. Because the Fathers do most seriously recommend the frequent recital
of the *Creed* to all faithfull Christians:
Amongst whom St. *Augustine* ; (some
of whose many pithy expressions upon
this point, we shal only here produce, to
avoid unnecessary prolixity) saies thus:
Having learned your *Creed*, recite it daily; when you rise out of your bed, when
you compose your selves to rest *&c.* Let
it not seem irksome to repeat it, Repetition is convenient, to avoid oblivion :
Do not pretend that you said it yester-
day, that you said it this day, that you
have it fresh in your memory ; but express it again, repeat it, contemplate it ;
let your *Creed* be your glass, there consider your selves & see whether you believe what you profess, and rejoyce daily
in your *Faith* : Let your Faith be your
riches, and let your *Creed* be (as it were)
the continual cloathing of your interiour. Do you not cloath your body
when you rise out of your Bead ? So by
reciting your *Symbol*, you cloath your
soul lest forgetfulness should leave it naked, *&c.*

An.

An Exercise upon the Apostles Creed:

I Believe.

I Believe, acknowledge, and confess with heart and mouth, all such Articles of Faith as the holy Church proposes to be believed, because God, (who is the Truth it self) hath revealed them.

In particular I believe all that is contained in the Apostles *Creed,* whereof I here make my profession in the presence of God my Creator, and all the Court of Heaven protesting and promising to live and dye in this Faith.

O Lord encrease my Faith !

I believe, (Lord !) help my unbelief.

I believe in God the Father Almighty,
Creator of Heaven and Earth.

I Believe in the first Person of the sacred Trinity, the eternal Father, whom *I* acknowledge to be full of all possible and imaginable might and power : and that he produced the Heaven, the Earth, and all Creatures both visible and invisible of *nothing,* by his sole word and command, and out of his own free-will and goodness.

O my

O my Almighty, and Almerciful Father! you can as easily bring me back into the dark Abyssmus of my first *Nothing*, as you from thence powerfullie drew me, and gave me this present *Being*; Behold, *I* most humbly acknowledge the absolute and perpetual dependance which *i* have upon your divine Majesty: *I* confess, that of my self *I* am nothing, have nothing, can do nothing; and that my whole Being, breathing, and motion, proceeds from your bounty, goodness, and power.

And in Jesus Christ his only Son, our Lord.

I Believe in the second Person of the sacred Trinity, the Son, whom the Father begot from all Eternity, communicating to him all his own Essence, Greatness, Perfection: who continuing God, became Man for the Salvation of Sinners; was named *Christ Jesus*, and is the Soveraign Lord and King of all Souls.

O divine word! which descended from Heaven to Earth, to deliver me from sin and *Satan*, be you my Lord by Election, as you are by Creation and Redemption. *I* freely give and bequeath my self to you for your perpetuall Bond-slave.

Live, O *Jesu*, and reign in my Soul, as you do in the whole extent of this large Universe.

Who was conceived by the Holy Ghost, born of the Virgin Mary.

I Believe that Gods Son, that he might become man, did vouchsafe to unite to his divine Person, a Rational soul and a humane body, which the Holy Ghost miraculously formed in the chaste bowels of the blessed Virgin *Mary*, and of her proper and pure blood: so that he was truly conceived in her, and truly born by her, without any prejudice to her Virginitie; O *Jesu*! the lover of Puritie, who chose the chastest woman of the World for your Mother : by the Immaculate Puritie of your Conception, and Nativitie, give me the gift and grace of purity of Life and Conversation.

Suffered under Pontius Pilate, was Crucified, dead, and buried.

I Believe that the Son of God Incarnate endured very severe Torments in his humanitie for the Worlds Redemption,

that he was adjudged to die by the President *Pilate* : and that after his death he
was buried and laid in a Sepulchre.

O *Jesu!* the Redeemer of my Soul!
your death is the only hope of my Life:
be you graciously pleased to apply to me
one single drop of your sacred Bloud,
and I shall rest secure in this Life, and be
happy for all Eternitie.

He descended into Hell, the third day he
arose again from the Dead.

I Believe that in the death of my blessed Saviour, his Soul was really separated for a time from his Body, to descend into that part of Hell which was
called *Limbus Patrum*, where all such
souls as from the Worlds first beginning
departed this life in a good estate, were
till then detained; I believe that he delivered them from that Dungeon, and
that upon the third day, his Soul returned to his buried Body, became reunited
unto it, and raised it up to Life and Immortality.

O most glorious Soul of Christ my
Saviour! which thus mercifully visited
the Patriarchs lying in the sad Prison of
Limbus: vouchsafe to give me also a gracious visit, that whilst I live, I may duly

and devoutly love and honour you: and when my Soul shall be called out of this imprisoning Body, it may be raised up to Contemplate, admire, and praise your greatness, goodness, and glorie, for all Eternity.

He ascended into Heaven, and sitteth at the right hand of God the Father Almightie.

I Believe that *Jesu* my Redeemer, being by his own power resuscitated from death to life, ascended up to Heaven by his own strength, where he sits at the right hand of God his Father (to whom he is every way equal) as the chief of all the Blessed, full of glory, and felicity.

O *Jesu*, my Redeemer! how worthy are you, thus to triumph, to reign, to be exalted above all Creatures! But O, forget not in the state of your greatness, the condition of your miserable Creature, bought with the price of your precious Blood! O King of glory! grant that all my thoughts, words, actions, and desires, may aym at nothing but your only honour.

From

From thence he shall come to judge the Quick and the Dead.

I Believe that Christ *Jesus* when he shall please to put a Period to time, and all sublunarie things will descend visibly from Heaven in his glorious Humanitie, to judge all Mankind, both the good and the bad, and publickly to reward or punish every one according to their works.

Ah ! just Judge of all consciences ! what shall I then do, or what shall I answer, when you shall question me concerning my whole lives transactions ?

I believe in the Holy Ghost.

I Believe in the third Person of the sacred Trinity, the *Holy Ghost,* who joyntly proceeds both from the Father and from the Son, and is to them equal in Greatness, in Majestie in all things whatsoever.

O sacred Spirit ! the God of Infinite Love and Charitie ! breath upon my flinty heart, mollifie it into meekness towards my Neighbour, and melt it into the sweet affections of your pure and perfect Love.

*I believe the Holy Catholick Church, the
Communion of Saints.*

I Believe the Catholick Church to be
the only Church of Christ ; that it is
holy, universal, apostolical, and infalli-
ble in things appertaining to Faith, and
that in this *Church* there are found many pious Souls, pleasing to the divine
Majesty, which mutually help each other
by their prayers and good works ! O
my Lord and my God ! I render you
most humble and hearty thanks for having made me a child and member of
this holy Church, in which I have so
great hopes, and so many helps to save
my soul : give me your grace (good *Jesus*) that I may improve this signal favour, and persever in this saving *Faith,*
that from it I may pass to the clear vision of your prepared glory.

The Forgiveness of Sins.

I Believe that God is both able and
willing to forgive me my Sins, and
that he hath left power in his *Church*
to remit them (be they never so heynous
and enormous) and this especiallie by
the Priests *absolution* in the Sacrament of

Penance. O God of Infinite goodnefs and mercy l let all Creatures Eternally praife and magnifie your facred Name, for having given *fuch power to men*, and fuch comfort to poor finners.

The Refurrection of the Flesh.

I Believe that the very body, in which my Soul now lives and breaths, and all humane bodies (though after death they are reduced into duft in their graves) fhall at the end of the World, and at the great day of general Judgment, be raifed to life, by Gods omnipotent command, and his Angels miniftry to be then rejoyned to their fame fouls, and to live for evermore.

O Dread Soveraign, in whofe hands are life and death, and to whofe beck all things are obedient ; Ingrave deeplie in my heart and foul the hope of a happie Refurrection, that the horrour of this temporal diffolution, and death of my body, may not over-terrifie and difmay me.

And life Everlasting, Amen.

I Believe that the good fhall live in Heavenlie glory for all Eternitie; and that the wicked shall live eternally in infernal torments. O good God I grant that I may so live in your grace during this my short Pilgrimage, that I may live with you in glorie, in your Eternal Paradise, *Amen.*

Of the Pater Noster, or our Lords Prayer. The second part of the Rosary.

THe *Pater Noster,* is the Prayer which our Lord *Jesus* taught his disciples, informing them from his own sacred mouth (and in them all Christians) how they should pray, and what they should beg daily of the divine Majestie.

It is the prime *Exemplar* of all Prayers, the *Abridgement* of the Gospel, the *Summary* of all our just and fitting petitions; and the absolute Form of imploring all such good things as we can expect and desire, and of deprecating all such bad things as we are to shun and avoid.

Finally, It is to be by so much the more zealously frequented, prized and reverenced before all other prayers whatsoever; by how much it excels them all in all sorts of prerogatives.

First, in Authority and dignity, as being prescribed by Christ *Jesus,* the

Wisdom it self, the *Truth* it self, the Divinity it self.

2. In Brevity and facility; as embracing in few, easie, and intelligible words, all that can rightly be demanded of the Divine Majestie.

3. In vertue and efficacy; For how should our heavenly Father refuse to hear our petitions which are humbly presented to his Throne of Mercy in the express terms, and in obedience to the precept of his dearly beloved Son Christ *Jesus*.

Affections contained in our Lords Prayer.

1. OF a poor *Pilgrim* and Prodigal *child*, sighing after his Country, kindred, and Fathers house: *Our Father which art in Heaven.*

2. Of a Faithful *servant*, forgetting himself to procure his Masters honour: *Hallowed be thy Name.*

3. Of a loving *Spouse*; desiring the sweet presence, embraces, and enjoyment of her beloved Bridegroom: *Thy Kingdome come.*

4. Of a dutiful *Son*; conforming himself absolutely to his Fathers sacred will and pleasure: *Thy will be done in earth as it is in Heaven.*

5. Of

5. Of a needy *Begger*, asking an Alms at the door of the Divine Mercy; *Give us this day our daily bread.*

6. Of a guilty *Prisoner*, deeply indebted, ready to be condemned, and petitioning for pardon and remission: *And forgive us our trespasses, as we forgive them that trespass against us.*

7. Of a Blind and weak *Traveller*, imploring light and strength that he err not, fall not, faint not in his journey: *And lead us not into temptation.*

8. Of a soul *Weary* of all things which hinder her desired perfection, and craving to be freed from them: *But deliver us from evil.*

An Exercise upon our Lords Prayer, Dilated with Acts and Affections.

1. Our Father which art in Heaven.

Adoration and acknowledgement.

O Heavenly Father! I no sooner had a Being, but I see the effects of your paternal Bountie, inflowing upon me all things necessary for my preservation, even to this present Instant, in
which

which I appear before your dread Majesty to adore you, praise you, and implore your Mercy.

I humbly acknowledge my own Ingratitude, Rebellion, Disobedience: all which notwithstanding, you have still continued the affection of a tender Father towards me, in cherishing me, comforting me, correcting me, pardoning me, protecting me, and treating me not as a Traytour, a Prodigal, a Slave, but as one of your dearly beloved Children.

Wherefore I *adore* you as my Soveraign Lord God, and I *honour* you, as my heavenly Father, and I *praise* you, as my powerful Creator, and I *love* you, as my merciful Preserver; and I *promise* for the future to *obey* you more punctually, to serve you more faithfully, to *praise* you more fervently, and to *procure* the dilatation of your divine honour and glorie more zealously upon all occasions, with a sincere, filial and cordial affection.

Hallowed be thy Name.

A desire of true light.

O what a Father! How full of pity, patience, compassion, to have so long en-

dured the undutifulness, irreverence, in-
solencie of an ill behaved, uncivil, unna-
tural child! who instead of procuring
the sanctification of your sacred *Name*
in all your creatures, and the exaltation
of your honour in all his actions, hath
still continued to dishonour your Majestie, to disedifie his Neighbour, to mis-
use your gifts, graces, and mercies; and
to defile his heart and soul with all sorts
of sins and impieties.

Grant, O Father of Light and Love!
that I may have a clear fight and lively
apprehension of your *affection*, and my
obligation: that truly considering your
mercy, and my own *misery*, I may relie
confidently upon *that*, and rise speedily
out of *this*: so recovering your favour
and friendship, and eternally sanctifying,
praising, and magnifying your sacred
Name and Majestie.

3: Thy Kingdom come.

Sorrow for our Sins, and sighing for Hea-
ven.

and quality; Permit me therefore to present my self before you as a poor *bond-slave*, or at least as the *Prodigal Child* with tears in my eyes, sighs in my heart, and this humble petition in my mouth.

Father! I have offended against Heaven, and before you: I have dissipated all the graces you so lovingly and liberally gave me, and forfeiting my whole freedom, am become the absolute slave of sensuality, vanity, impiety, which now over-rule me, raigh within me, and render me a rebel against your divine Majestie.

Mercie, O most compassionate Father! Destroy this Kingdom of Sin and Satan, and Establish yours in my soul! Live Lord Jesu in my heart! I will have no other King but him.

Deprive me not (Dear Father!) of that happy inheritance, which your Son my Saviour hath purchased for me with the price of his precious blood; but mercifully grant that your glorious Kingdom may come to be my lot and portion, at my departure out of this place of banishment; that I may there contemplate, praise, and love you for evermore.

4. Thy will be done in Earth as it is in Heaven.

Efficacious Purpose and Resolution of self-denial.

I Desire no longer, O Eternal Father! to follow my irregular appetites, and to match under the Banner of my own will and opinion, which are the fountains of all my defects, disloyalties, transgressions: No Lord! For your love, I utterly renounce them with all possible horrour and hatred.

All my will, and wish is, that your sacred will may be accomplished in *me* upon *Earth*, in *Heaven*, in *all* things whatsoever, purely, perfectly, eternallie; for all your Ordinances are full of Justice and equity; I adore them all; I embrace them all; I submit to them all.

Thrice happy those souls which are truly conformable to you, which incessantly contemplate you, which unweariedly follow you, which faithfully serve you, and perpetually praise you.

5. Give us this day our daily Bread.

Petition for a supply of our Necessities.

IT is the property of *Children* oppressed with hunger, to address themselves to their *Parents* with tears and cries, to move them to compassion: Behold here your poor Child, O loving and liberal Lord God! extreamly labouring with spiritual thirst and hunger, exceedingly wearied in the worlds service: you are my Father, my Feeder, my daily Bread; And it is you only who are capable to satisfie my hunger, quench my thirst, comfort me in this my calamitous condition; All *Creatures* are but small *Crums* falling from your Royal table.

O how sweet and savory is the *Bread* of tears, and the *Water* of contrition to a truly Penitent, Contrite, Converted Soul! Your sugred words (O Lord!) and your celestial inspirations are her most delicious sawce, and the participation of your most precious Body and Blood, her daily Bread.

O my God! Let not the affection to temporal objects, deprive me of spiritual comforts; nor let any earthly solicitudes and greediness after worldlie goods choak up the memorie and gust of those better goods you have promised and prepared for me in Heaven.

But let my dailie Exercise be to sanctifie your holie *Name* ; Let the interiour feeling of your *Kingdom* of Love in my foul, be my only pleasure, palace, and Paradise ; and let the accomplishment of your sacred *Will*, be my dailie Bread and sustenance, during the space of this my Pilgimage.   But alas !

6. Forgive us our trespasses, as we forgive them that trespass against us.

Reflection upon our Impieties, and Supplication for pardon.

WHen I consider, O Father of infinite Clemencie ! not only my life past, but even my present condition; not only all my enormous and innumerable offences, but even my dailie and hourlie imperfections, negligences, iniquities, to wit,

1. My time still lost, either in doing *Evill*, or in doing *nothing*, or in doing things *impertinent*.

2. My lingring and voluntarie com-

placencies in thought against Chastitie, Chastitie, Humilitie.|

3. My continued Resistencie, contristation, hinderance of your holy spirit In my self or others,

4. My Irreverence, Indevotion, Tepiditie in my prayers, recollections, spiritual Exercises.

5. My Excesses of Tongue, Eyes, Ears, and all my senses, as well in respect of your divine Majestie, as my neighbour, and my self.

When (I say) I seriouslie reflect upon these and the rest of my manifold transgressions, I find my self so deeplie indebted, that I should undoubtedlie turn Bankrupt, did not your fatherlie goodness, and my deer Redeemers boundless mercie and merits give me hope, comfort, and encouragement:

For, O my God! In what large sum do I stand ingaged to your sacred Justice.

1. I owe *thanks* for so many signal Benefits.

2. I owe *Contrition* for so many committed Crimes.

3. I owe *love*, for love; my *life* for your Sons death; my whole *self*, for your self given, and regiven so frequentlie unto me.

And yet, insensible wretch that I am! I pay none of these just *debts*, but daylie increase my obligations by my dailie *Ingratitude*.

What other course then can I now take, but humblie to cry out, *Dimitte mihi*: Pardon your prodigal Child (O compassionate Father!) for the love of your dear Son Christ *Jesus*: He is my suretie, and he hath satisfied for my debts, even according to the severe rigour of your divine Justice, whose least drop of bloud is abundantlie sufficient to expiate the whole Worlds impieties.

If therefore my own *guilt* shuts up my mouth, and your Mercie gate; yet his sacred *bloud* will be my *Key* to open both the one and the other. Pardon me then (O my pious Father!) for your Crucified *Jesus* sake, as I for the love of him, do most freelie, heartilie, and sincerelie pardon all them who have injured, wronged, and offended me in any thing whatsoever.

G 7. And

7. And lead us not into temptation.

Recourse to the divine Protection.

I Am day and night, (O most Powerful Father and Protector!) assaulted
with an infinite number of *Enemies*,
which incessantlie seek my utter ruine
and destruction: The *flesh* charmes me,
the *world* enchants me, the *Devill* cheats
me, and *every thing* becomes an object
of Temptation unto me.

Ah! How shall poor I conquer such
powerful champions? I find no other
means, than to make my addresses to
you (My all-powerful Father!) and
humbly to shelter my self under the
wings of your paternal Protection.

For alas! such is my frailtie, that I
shall surelie *fall* without the support of
your Grace; *being fall'n*, I shall be un-
able to *rise* without the help of your
strength; *being raised up*, I cannot hope
to *persevere* without the continual in-
fluence of your assistance.

Shield me then under your sacred
wings; Protect me as the Apple of
your eye; command your Angel of
light to preserve me from the darkness

of Sin, from the dangers of my Adversaries, from the dismal sleep of sudden
and unprovided death, from all that is
any way displeasing to your divine will
and liking.

8. But deliver us from evill.

Aspirations to perfection, fruition, union.

WHen (O Father of Glorie!) shall
I be freed from sin, from Sa-
than, from my self, from all that hinders
the coming of your Kingdom?

O Kingdom of Peace, Kingdom of
love, Kingdom of all desirable felicitie!
There it is (O Father!) that I shall *sanctifie your Name,* that I shall *perform your
will,* purely, perfectly, eternallie.

There I shall no longer beg of you
my daily Bread, but remain abundantlie
satiated with the light of your blessed
face, and the fruition of your beatifying
glorie.

There *my Debts* will be all paid, my
sins pardoned, my soul glorified.

There, will be neither *Temptation,*
nor Tribulation; neither occasion of sin,
nor punishment of sin, but all tranquilli-
tie, all conformitie, all perfection.

There lives thy loving Father (O my

Soul ') There is thy home and Countrey, there lies thy portion and patri-
monie.

O *Jerusalem*, my dear Countrey, my
delicious Kingdom, my desired *Inheri-*
tance, when shall *I* possess thee? O
sweet Father! when shall *I* sincerely
love you! O my poor Soul! when shall
I see thee free from stains and blemishes,
full of puritie and perfection?

Let's yield, let's yield to our good Father: Let's promptly submit to all his
precepts, and Ordinances; Let's serve
him with a filial reverence, obedience,
confidence; that we may *here* feel the
affects of his Grace, and *hereafter* enjoy
the priviledges of his Glorie.

Of the Ave Marie, or, Angelical Sa-
lutation.

The third part of the Rosary.

THere is no question amongst all
faithful Christians; but that the
Pater and *Ave* are the two most excellent Prayers we have (as St. *Thomas*
largely proves) and consequentlie that
they are of greatest efficacie to obtain
what we want and desire : The *one*
being delivered and dictated by the

divine Month of Gods own Son our Redeemer Christ *Jesus:* The *other*, being pronounced by an Archangel, sent Ambassador from the sacred Trinity to *Her* who was chosen out amongst all women, to be the worthy Mother of the second divine Person, the Word Eternal. And who can doubt, but that *God himself* is also the Author of this *Salutation*, and that he put this *lesson* into his Legats mouth, whom surely he sent well instructed in all things which might concern his weighty Embassie?

Let us therefore briefly declare the use and scope of this short, sweet, and mysterious *Salutation* and *Prayer*; and afterwards dilate it with Acts and Affections; that it being so often to be repeated in the recital of the *Rosary*, may give more gust to their devotion, who will sometimes take the time and leisure to ruminate upon it more diligently.

There is surely nothing more befitting a faithful Christian, than a frequent Reflexion upon his *Redemption*; And since the *Incarnation* of Gods Son in the sacred Virgins womb, is the *chief Mystery* thereof, we must needs conclude, That it is an office of Piety most grateful to the divine Majesty, to revolve often *those very words*, whereby so great a

Myftery (fo long expected, fo ardently defired, fo zealoufly begg'd by the holy people of all precedent ages) was firft announced to mankind; efpecially it being directly intended, as a thankful and dutiful commemoration of the fignal benefit of our *Redemption*, and our Saviours *Incarnation*.

The *Ave Maria* (fays our devout St. *Bernard*) is of fuch power and excellencie, That it caufes Heaven to fmile, the Angels to be glad, the Devils to flie away, and Hell to fear and tremble, as often as it is reverently recited.

After whom, faid another of the B. Virgins Minions *Alanus*, The *Ave Mary* is a prayer little in words but large in Myfteries; it is fhort in difcourfe, but fublime in fenfe and vertue; it is fweet above honie, and precious beyond the pureft gold.

Liften faies he, with admiration to what I fhall here tell, O you true Lovers of *Mary's* name and honour.

All Heaven rejoyceth, and the whole Earth is aftonifhed, when I fay *Ave Maria*.

Sathan avoids, and Hell trembles, when I fay *Ave Maria*.

The world becomes contemptible, and my heart melts into inward affections.

ons, when I say *Ave Maria*. All fear is
banished, and the Flesh is conquered,
when I say *Ave Maria*.

Devotion arises, compunction encrea-
ses, when I say, *Ave Maria*.
Faith is strengthened, Hope redoubled,
Charity enflamed, comfort renewed, the
Spirit recreated, when I say *Ave Maria*.

This *Angelical Salutation* may be said
to have *three* parts, as it hath *three* Authors, though all inspired from God,
the Prime Author, and Origin thereof.

The *First* part ; (*Hail Mary full of
grace, our Lord is with thee, blessed art
thou amongst women*) was delivered by
the Angel *Gabriel*, as it is recorded in
the 2. chap. of St. *Luke*, verse 28.

The *second* part ; (*and blessed is the fruit
of thy womb, Jesus !*) was pronounced
by St. *Elizabeth* the holy Baptists Mother, *Luke* 2. verse 42.

The third part ; (*Holy Mary, Mother
of God, pray for us sinners now, and at the
hour of our death*) was added by the Catholick Church, in the general Council
of *Ephesus*, and recommended to the
use of all Christians, in opposition of
Nestor, and other hereticks, who denied
the blessed Virgin to be Gods Mother.

The *first* and *second* part of this Salutation were frequently made use of

open

even from the first Infancy of Christia-
nity, (as appears by the Liturgy of St.
James, receiv'd in the sixth general
Council: and the *third* part ever since
the general Council of *Ephesus*.

The affections contain'd in the Hail Mary,
or Angelical Salutation.

1. Of Congratulation, *Hail Mary.*
2. Of Exultation, *Full of Grace.*
3. Of Admiration, *our Lord is with
thee.*
4. Of Benediction, *Blessed art thou
amongst women; and blessed is the fruit of
thy womb,* Jesus !

Whereby we bless and praise both the
Mother and the Son, we beg both their
blessings, and desire all creatures to bless,
praise and honour them both.

5. Of Invocation and Petition, foun-
ded upon her *Power*, she being Gods
Mother; *Holy Mary, Mother of God,
pray for us sinners now, and at the hour of
our death.*

An Explication of the Hail Mary, *or the
the Angelical Salutation.*

Hail.

That is, be you glad, joyful, secure
and happy, in being made the prime Instrument

ſtrument of Gods providence and mercy, in order to our *Redemption,* and to the changing of our Mother *Eves* hereditary curſe into a happy bleſſing for all ſucceeding generations.

Mary.

Is the proper name of the glorious Mother of *Jeſus,* ſignifying, Lady and Star of the Sea.

Full of grace.

As being full of God, by her ſpecial priviledge of conceiving the Word Eternal, and conſequently full of all vertue, goodneſs, and perfection whatſoever.

Our Lord is with thee.

For *God the Father* in a moſt ſingular manner over-ſhadowed her, *God the Holy Ghoſt* moſt abundantly came upon her, and *God the Son* moſt wonderfully became man within her.

The *Father* was with her, as with his Daughter: the *Son* was with her, as with his Mother: the *Holy Ghoſt* was with her, as with his dearly beloved Spouſe, and choyceſt Tabernacle.

Bleſſed

Blessed art thou amongst Women.

That is, over, above, and beyond all women, because a *Mother* and a *Virgin*: the *Mother* of God, which is above all other humane Titles, and yet a perpetual *Virgin*, a priviledge which never any other creature did, or shall possess.

And blessed is the fruit of thy womb, Jesus.

Who remaining perfect God, evermore blessed in his divine Person, became perfect man in her sacred womb, to whom we give all possible praise, homage, and gratitude, for all that we have and are, and especially for this his cloathing himself with our humane nature in her, whereby he truly becomes our *Brother*, and provides her for our powerful Mother.

Holy Mary, Mother of God, pray for us sinners now, and at the hour of our death.

We make to her our humble addresses in all our pressing necessities, that by Her we may receive what we want, by whom we receiv'd the Author himself of all goodness.

An Exercise upon the Ave Mary, dilated with Acts, &c.

Hail Mary.

All Hail ! the most holy, excellent, and admirable of all pure creatures ! Princess of Heaven and Earth ! Queen of Men and Angels ! I desire now to salute you with the reverence of the Archangel *Gabriel,* with the affection of St. *Elizabeth,* with the devotion of the holy Church, and with all such honour as is due to Gods sacred Mother.

I salute you, admire you, congratulate you, O amiable Virgin-Mother *Mary* ! as the chief instrument of our Redemption, the prime Ornament of Paradise, the singular Glory of humane nature, and the bright Star shining unto us by your exemplary Vertues, and directing us by your powerful assistance in this sea of miseries, and place of Pilgrimage.

Full of Grace.

I salute you, O most sacred, pure and perfect Virgin-Mother ! as *full of Grace* from the first instant of your immaculate Conception : *full of sanctity,* during the
whole

whole course of your unspotted life upon earth: *full of glory* in the happy state of your Eternity in Heaven.

O most Powerful, and most Compassionate Virgin-Mother! out of this your plenitude of grace, vertue, sanctity, and perfection, impart what you see wanting to my poor needy, and naked Soul.

Our Lord is with thee.

Our Lord God, was, is, and will be evermore with you, O Virgin-Mother! and you are, and always shall be with him: He was with you upon Earth, in your womb, in your arms, at your breasts: He *is with you* in Heaven, by his beatifying presence, he *will be* there still *with you*, bestowing on you a continued Eternity of glory.

O most unspotted Temple of the sacred Trinity! by this your perpetual and perfect union with the Divinity, obtain for me that I may pass on this my Pilgrimage in the daily exercise, and reflection upon the divine presence, to the end I may with you be perpetually united to him hereafter in his happy Paradise.

Blessed

Blessed art thou amongst women.

O *Mary!* the only Mother amongst all Virgins!

O *Mary!* the only Virgin amongst all Mothers! you conceiv'd without Sin, brought forth without sorrow, liv'd without blemish, and after your death were translated to Eternal glory, without the least touch of corruption; therefore *blessed are you above all women*, who were totally exempted from the common curses of all other women.

You bore him in your womb, who bears up the whole world: you infolded him in your arms, who encompasses the spacious frame of the vast Universe: you nourish'd him with your breast-milk, who gives Being, life, food to all Creatures. Finally, you were, and are Gods Mother: in which miraculous word is included all the priviledges and perfections, which can possibly befall a creature, and therefore you are justly stil'd, and shall be so esteem'd by all succeeding generations, *the most blessed of all womankind*: O blessed *Mary*, the Paragon of all Mothers, the Crown of all Virgins, the joy of all the Saints, the best and most accomplish'd of all Gods

Creatures I by these, and all other your
numberless Benedictions, avert from me
those maledictions which I have deser-
vedly incurr'd by my enormous sins and
transgressions.

And blessed is the fruit of thy womb, Jesus.

O *Jesu!* the sacred fruit of *Maries*
virginal body! be your Name and Majesty eternally blessed by all creatures in
Heaven and upon Earth.

Blessed be your divine *Person*, which
you thus vouchsafed to unite unto a humane body and soul for the Worlds Salvation.

Blessed be your *Will*, which was thus
instam'd with the love of lost Mankind.

Blessed be your *Memory*, which mercifully reflected upon us miserable and
caitiff creatures.

Blessed be your *Understanding*, your
Wisdome, your *Power*, your *Providence*,
and all your ineffable *Attributes*, which
found out such an efficacious way to
win us to your self, and wed us to your
sweet affection and friendship.

O Amiable *Jesu!* the ornament of
the Universe, the Beauty of Heaven, the
Glory of Mankind; Be you *blessed* in
each member, part and particle of your

most pure, immaculate, virginal Body, which you expos'd to such cruel torments for our Redemption.

By these and all other the infinite blessings which are in you, and belong to you: (sweet *Jesu!*) bestow on me the blessing of your grace in this my lives Pilgrimage, and of your glory in your Eternal Paradise.

Holy Mary, *Mother of God, pray for us sinners now, and at the hour of our death.*

O blessed Mother of blessed *Jesus!* despise not them for whom the dear Son of your womb, disdain'd not to die upon the Cross: but in your tender pitie and compassion succour the miserable, encourage the weaklings, comfort the afflicted, and let all such feel the happy effects of your helping assistance, as have recourse to your powerful Prayers and Patronage.

We beseech you, O gracious Mother! by all the greatnesses which God hath given you, by the glorious Name of *Mary,* and *Title* of Gods Mother wherewith he hath honoured you, by the singular love he bore you upon Earth, and the supereminent glory wherewith he hath crown'd you Queen of Heaven; Pray *now* for us, that we may pass on the short remainder of our lives Pilgrimage in his grace and favour; and when *Death* shall summon us to depart out of this miserable World; Then, O then (most charitable Mother!) chiefly assist, encourage, and strengthen us, your poor children, and conduct our Souls to the happy mansions which your divine Son, our dear Redeemer, hath before all time prepar'd for them in his Heavenly Kingdom, where with you (O most glorious Queen-Mother!) they shall see him, enjoy him, and be united to him for all Eternity.

If we would thus devoutly reflect sometimes upon these or the like mystical *senses, and raise up our Souls to such like affections, when we recite these divine forms of Prayer, we should probably reap more Spiritual* profit *by their frequent repetition.*

But we therefore take little or no gust in these and other pious Exercises, *and make small progress in perfection, because we commonly content our selves with the bark and bare out-side of the words, and seldom or never penetrate into their inward marrow, sense, and meaning.*

Sect.

SECTION VII.

The manner how to recite the Rosary.

1. IN the *first* place you are to settle your self reverentlie in the *divine presence,* and (seriously recollecting your senses) to cast off all evagations of mind, and extroversions, (which is the *general* preparation to all Prayer.)

2. To the end your *understanding* and *will* (both which concur in all well-ordered Prayer and Meditation) may be profitably employed; you may please to remember these *two Rules.*

The *First Rule* (which concerns the action of your understanding) is, *To represent before the Eyes of your Soul that mystery, whereon you are to meditate, as even then acted in your presence.*

As for Example, The mysterie whereupon you intend to make your meditation, is, *The Nativitie of our Saviour;* Imagine your self standing in a private corner of the poor *Bethleem* Stable, beholding, hearing, and admiring all that there passed in that sacred night: run over in your mind the condition of the place, and the circumstances of the *Persons*, and think what were their *thoughts*, affections, words, actions: above all consider *who it was*, that appeared to the World in this mean equipage: to wit, the Son of God, the King of Glorie, the Monarch of the whole Universe: then ponder his love to mankind in general, and to your self in particular, *&c.*

The *second Rule* (which concerns the action of your will) is, *That you pass speedily from speculative discourses to devout Affections, and self reflections,* As for example, had you been in the *Bethleem* stable aforesaid, how diligentlie would you have employed your self in the service of little *Jesus*, and his loving *Mother?* How willinglie would you have picked up sticks, made a fire, ayred his swaths, and fetched or carried whatsoever might have been useful for their solace and succour, *&c.*

Such like reflections will raise enflamed desires, and firm resolutions in your soul, of better loving and serving both the Son and Mother for the future, and of suffering for his sake, who suffered so much for yours, *&c.*

And in some such manner you may conclude each *mystery* by some particular resolution (drawn from the subject of the *meditation*) either of correcting such an imperfection, or of exercising such a vertue : and assure your self, that if you presently apply your self to the practice of such well made resolutions, (humbly imploring the divine assistance therein by the blessed Virgins Intercession :)you shall find it a most speedy and efficacious means to the amendment of your life, the extirpation of vice, the implanting of vertue ; and finallie much conducing to your general advancement in all sorts of spiritual Perfections.

3. You may also represent to your self the sacred Virgin:

Sometimes as sitting or kneeling in her silent and solitarie retreat, and attentively listning to the Angel *Gabriels* Salutation and Embassy.

Other times, as infolding gentlie her sweet Infant *Jesus* in her sacred arms, imbracing him tenderlie in her bosome, suckling him lovinglie at her breasts, watching him carefullie with her eyes, cherishing him affectionatlie with her kisses, contemplating him devoutly with her heart.

Other times as painfullie waiting on him from place to place in the time of his *Passion*, sorrowfullie standing by him at the foot of his Cross, cheerfullie rejoycing with him at his *Resurrection.*

Other times, as glorioufly reigning in Heaven, mercifully vouchfafing to hearken to our prayers, and piously prefenting them to her Son.

Or otherwife according to the feveral myfteries, and futably to each ones guft and devotion.

4. You are alfo here to be exhorted to propofe to your felf the caufe (whether common or particular) which moves you now to the recital of the Rofary: As for example, I intend now to praife my Lord God for the benefit of my Creation, Redemption, Vocation *&c.* Or in the honour of my Saviours facred Nativitie, bitter Paffion, glorious Refurrection, admirable Afcention *&c,* Or in the honour of the bleffed Virgins Annunciation, Vifitation, Affumption, Coronation, *&c.* Or I intend to render thanks to my Creator for fuch a particular favour as for mine own, or my friends Converfion, delivery from danger, *&c.* or any other private or publick benefit, Or, I intend to implore the divine affiftance for the overcoming of fuch a *Temptation,* extirpating fuch a *vice,* obtaining fuch a *vertue.* Or, For a good fuccefs in fuch an affair; Or, that I may make a happy progrefs in my Stu-

Consider therefore briefly at the beginning of your prayers, *what it is* that you chiefly intend : and if it be any temporal or worldly benefit which you desire to obtain, be sure you demand it not *absolutely,* but only *conditionally,* as thus : If it please the divine Majestie, and that it is for my good and his glory : I humbly beg a happy end of such a Law-sute: success in such a journey, prosperity in such an undertaking, &c.

5. Then taking your *Bedes* in hand, or having this your *Book* open before you : begin your *Rosary* with the sign of the *Cross:* saying, In the name of the Father, and of the *Son,* and of the Holy Ghost, *Amen.*

6. Then adding this *Preparatorie Prayer of the Church,* Aperi Domine os me-um, &c.

O Lord! Open my mouth to bless your holy name, purge my heart from all vain, wicked, and wandring thoughts: enlighten my understanding, and inflame my affections: that (reciting this Rosary, with due reverence, attention, and devotion,)

1. For the increase of your honour and glory.

2. For the Exaltation of the Catho-

3. For the Prosperitie of the *Sea Apostolick.*

4. For the peace of all Christian Princes.

5. For the re-union of *Schismaticks.*

6. For the Conversion of *Hereticks.*

7. For the Correction of *Sinners.*

8. For the Consolation of the afflicted both living and departed.

9. For the preservation of our *Soveraign,* Queen *Catherine,* and all the devout Rosarists of this holy Confraternity; I may be graciously heard by your divine Majesty: through the merits of your *Son,* our Lord and Saviour Christ Jesus.

7. *Then making a Profession of your Faith, with heart and mouth, say.*

I believe in God the Father Almightie Creator of Heaven and Earth, *&c.*

8. *After your Creed recite thrice your* Hail Mary, *upon the three grains which are commonly placed at the head of your* Rosary, *saluting the blessed Virgin, in honour of her three singular Prerogatives.*

Of being
1. The Daughter of the Eternal Father.
2. The Mother of the Eternal Son.
3. The Spouse of the Holy Ghost.

9. *Then Reflecting upon the first my-* sterie: say, Our Father, and ten Hail Maries, *and so pass on to the second, and the rest of the* Decades, *according to the order hereafter described: and in the end of every* Decade you are to say, Glory be to the Father, and to the *Son*, and to the Holy Ghost. As it was in the beginning, is now, and ever shall be, World without end, *Amen.*

Then recite these Verses devoutly.

These Prayers Angelical with bended
  knee,
We offer holy Virgin up to thee;
Steer us a prosperous course while here
  we tarry.
And in deaths Pangs assist us blessed
  Mary.
Remember Virgin that no Age hath
  known,
Any by thee deserted, that has flown
To thy Protection, or implor'd thy Aid,
By which encouragement, most sacred
  Maid,
Mother of Virgins, I to thee repair,
And for thy help address my humble
  Prayer,
Mother of God! desert me not, but
  hear,
And listen to me with a gracious ear.

10. *And having compleated the Recital of your Rosary, conclude with the repeated* Creed *and sign of the* Cross : (*so ending where you began*) *which is both the ancient, and a most laudable custome,*

After all, add this Prayer of the Church, to obtain the remission of all the negligences commited in your Prayers.

Sacrosanctæ & individuæ Trinitati, &c.

To the sacred and undivided Trinitie, to the blessed Humanitie of our crucified Lord Jesus, to the fruitful integritie of the most glorious Virgin *Mary*, and to all the *Saints* universally be ascribed all praise, honour, and glory, from all creatures for evermore; and to us be granted (by Gods Mercy) the Remission of all our Sins.

And likewise, ever blessed be the *Bowels* of the Virgin *Mary*, which bore the Eternal Fathers Son : and blessed be the *Breasts* which suckled Christ our Lord; *Amen.*

SECTION VIII.

An Explication of the formal parts of the Rosary ;

WHich are the fifteen Mysteries answering to the fifteen Decades, or Tens of the sacred *Rosary*; and here set down in that direct order which ought to be observ'd in meditating upon them : which is, First to begin with the five joyful mysteries. Secondly, to proceed to the five Dolorous. Thirdly, to conclude with the five Glorious ; for according to this order they were accomplish'd in the Persons of our Saviour Christ, and his blessed Mother.

The five joyful Mysteries, (so called, for that they contain the chief joys which the sacred Virgin-Mother felt concerning her Son Christs humane nature;) Are,

1. The Annunciation of Christs Incarnation, by the Archangel *Gabriel,* *Luke* I.

2. The Visitation which the B. Virgin made to her Cousin St. *Elizabeth,* *Luke* I.

3. The

3. The Nativitie of our Lord Jesus Christ, *Luke* 2.

4. The Oblation and Presentation of our Saviour Christ to his Eternal Father in the Temple; and the Purification of his B. Mother, *Luke* 2.

5. The finding of Christ in the Temple, disputing with the Doctors, when he was twelve yeers old.

The five dolorous mysteries (so called, for that they contain the chief sorrows which Christ our Redeemer felt in his bitter Passion;) *Are*,

1. The bloudy Agonie of Christ, whilest he was at his Prayers in the garden, *Math.* 26.

2. His most cruel Flagellation, or whipping at the Pillar, *John* 19.

3. The crowning of his Head with thorns, *Mat.* 27.

4. The carrying of his Cross to mount *Calvary, John* 19.

5. His crucifixion and death upon the Cross, *John* 19. *Luke* 23. *Mark* 15. *Mat.* 27.

The five glorious mysteries, (so called, for that they contain the chief glories which befel our Saviour Christ and his sacred Mother,) Are,

1. The Resurrection of our Lord Jesus, *Mark* 16.

2. His Ascension into Heaven, *Mar.* 16

3. His sending down the Holy Ghost
to his Church, *Acts* 2.

4. The Assumption of the B. Virgin
Mary up to Heaven.

5. The Coronation of the B. Virgin
in Heaven.

Which fifteen Mysteries are briefly
comprehended in three Verses.

She's told, She visits, He's born, offered and found.

He prays, is whipp'd, is crown'd, carries, is kill'd.

Rises, Ascends, sends down: she dies,
is crown'd.

SECTION IX.

A Practical way to say the Rosary.

*The 1. Part, containing the five
joyful mysteries.*

The first Joyful Mystery, To wit,
The Annunciation.
[*She's Told.*]

UNder this one notion, are comprehended many particular joys, where-

with the sacred Virgins soul was replenished, upon the happy news brought down to her from heaven, of the Eternal Word's Incarnation in her womb; which we shall (both here and in the following mysteries) reduce to ten heads, according to the number of Angelical salutations, recited in each Decad; that so the pious Rosarist may entertain his devotion by mentally ruminating upon one, or more, or all of them, as his leisure shall permit, and his zeal suggest unto him: Thus,

In the name of the Father, &c.

O Lord open my mouth, &c.

I believe in God, &c. with three times *Hail Mary.*

Our Father &c.

Then he may consider the joy of the B. Virgins heart.

1. At her eternal pre-election; that she amongst all women, should be chosen to be the Mother of Gods son, &c.

Hail Mary.

2. At her singular benediction, *Blessed art thou, &c.* (said the Archangel,) *Luke 2.*

Hail Mary.

3. At the reparation of mankind, whereunto she was made instrumental.

Hail M.

4. At the Angelical salutation ; That she should be thus particularly and honorably saluted by such an Ambassador.
Hail Mary.

5. At the Angelical Consolation, Fear nothing, O *Mary, Luke 2.*
Hail Mary.

6. At the Angelical Revelation, *Behold thou shalt conceive, &c.*
Hail Mary.

7. At the Angelical Instruction, *How can this be ? The Holy Ghost shall descend upon thee, &c.*
Hail Mary.

8. At her being with child of the Word Incarnate.
Hail Mary.

9. At the manner of her conceiving; without the knowledge of man, &c.
Hail Mary.

10. At her marriage with St *Joseph.*
Hail Mary.

Glory be to the Father, &c.
These Praiers Angelical, &c.

The second joyful Mystery ; To wit, The Visitation.
[*She Visits.*]

Our Father, &c.
The B. Virgin exceedingly rejoyced.

1. At the confideration of Gods wonderful works now revealed unto her by this Heavenly meſſenger.

Hail Mary.

2. At the Inhabitation of God within her.

Hail Mary.

3. At her perfect Sanctification.

Hayl Mary.

4. At her ſingular Illuſtration both in ſoul and body.

Hail Mary.

5. At her journey into *Judea.*

Hail Mary.

6. At the carriage of Chriſt in her womb.

Hail Mary.

7. At the bleſſing of *Elizabeth.*

Hail Mary.

8. At her conjoyn'd Virginity and Maternity.

Hail Mary.

9. At the overflowing of her Grace into *St. John, Elizabeth,* and *Zachary.*

Hail Mary.

10. At the many miracles accompanying and following this Viſitation.

Hail Mary.

Glory be to the Father, &c.

Theſe Prayers Angelical, &c.

The third joyful Mystery; To wit,
the Nativity of our Lord Jesus.
[*He's Born.*]

Our Father, &c.
The B. Virgin exceedingly rejoyced.

1. At the first sight of her new born
Jesus.
Hail Mary.
2. At her preserv'd Virginity.
Hail Mary.
3. At her bringing forth without pain.
Hail Mary.
4. At the Angelical Jubilation.
Hail Mary.
5. At the vision of the divine Essence.
Hail Mary.
6. At the many benefits bestowed on
Man-kind by her Sons Birth.
Hail Mary.
7. At the multitude of miracles
wrought then for his manifestation to
the World.
Hail Mary.
8. At the Adoration of the Wise-
men.
Hail Mary.
9. At their mystical offerings.

10. At the Vocation, Conversion, and Salvation of the Gentiles.

Hail Mary.
Glory be to the Father, &c.
These Prayers Angelical, &c.

The fourth joyful Mystery ; To wit, His Oblation.
[*Offe'd.*]

Our Father, &c.
The B. Virgin exceedingly rejoyced.

1. At the carriage of her sweet Son Jesus, from *Bethleem* to *Jerusalem.*
Hail Mary.
2. At the compleating of former Prophecies.
Hail Mary.
3. At the offering up of her Son.
Hail Mary.
4. At her exemption from the Law of Purification.
Hail Mary.
5. At the instruction and example of her Sons Humility and Obedience.
Hail Mary.
6. At the wonderful Manifestation and revelation of her Son ; To wit, Not only to St. *Joseph*, St. *Zachary*, St.

Elizabeth, the *Shepherds,* and the *Kings,* but now alſo to St. *Simeon* and St. *Anne* in the Temple.

Hail Mary.

7. At Venerable *Simeons* receiving her Son into his arms.

Hail Mary.

8. At the Bleſſing of *Simeon.*

Hail Mary.

9. At the like Devotion, Jubilation, and Illumination of St. *Anne.*

Hail Mary.

10. At the ſignification and fruit of this Oblation.

Hail Mary.

Glory be to the Father, &c.
Theſe Prayers Angelical, &c.

The fifth joyful Myſtery; To wit,
The finding of Chriſt in the
Temple.
[*And Found.*]

Our Father, &c.
The B. Virgin-Mother exceedingly rejoyced.

1. At the ſight of her now found Son.

Hail Mary.

2. At the hearing of his Learning and Wiſdome.   *Hail Mary.*

3. At the fulfilling of that Propheti-cal saying, *I Wisedom dwell with Counsel, and am present amongst learned cogita-tions.*

Hail Mary.

4. At her first conference with him after she had found him.

Hail Mary.

5. At his Mystical answer unto her.

Hail Mary.

6. At the Instruction couched in his reply.

Hail Mary.

7. At his return with her to *Nazareth.*

Hail Mary.

8. At his humble Obedience and Subjection.

Hail Mary.

9. At the consideration of her own happiness, dignity and excellency.

Hail Mary.

10. At the delicious conservation of all his words and actions in her heart.

Hail Mary.

Glory be to the Father, &c.

These Prayers Angelical, &c.

I believe in God, &c.

To the sacred and undivided Tri-nity, &c.

The

The second Part of the Rosary, containing the Five Dolorous Mysteries.

Begin this part of the Rosary with the Prayer, sign of the Cross, and Creed, as in the first part.

In the name of the Father, &c.
O Lord open my mouth, &c.
I believe in God &c.

The first Dolorous Mystery.
[He Prays.]

Our Father, &c.
Our Blessed Saviour was exceedingly sad and sorrowful.

1. At the apprehension of the loss of his corporal life.
   Hail Mary.
2. At the foresight of his sufferings.
   Hail Mary.
3. At the consideration of the heynousness of Sin.
   Hail Mary.
4. At the Jews Ingratitude.

ans would reap from his Paſſion.

Hail Mary.

6. At the Treaſon of *Judas.*

Hail Mary.

7. At the Scandal, ſcattering, and flight of his deareſt Diſciples, friends, and followers.

Hail Mary.

8. At his being taken, bound, and brought out of the Garden of Mount Olivet.

Hail Mary.

9. At his preſentation to *Annas* and *Caiphas,* and the ſuborning of falſe wit-neſſes againſt him.

Hail Mary.

10. At his Blows, Buffets, and other opprobrious uſage, all night long.

Hail Mary.

Glory be to the Father, &c.

Theſe Prayers Angelical, &c.

The ſecond Dolorous Myſtery.
[*Is Whipp'd.*]

Our Father, &c.

Our Bleſſed Saviour was exceeding-ly afflicted.

1. At his Preſentation to *Pilate.*

Hail Mary.

2. At his ſtanding before a Pagan

Judge, in quality of a notorious Criminal.

Hail Mary.

3. At the Jews false accusations,

Hail Mary.

4. At his being sent to *Herod.*

Hail Mary.

5. At *Herods* scorn, and contempt,

Hail Mary.

6. At the peoples clamour, to have *Barabbas* pardon'd, and Christ put to death.

Hail Mary.

7. At his most cruel and contumelious whipping.

Hail Mary.

8. At his being stripp'd naked before the whole multitude,

Hail Mary.

9. At the stretching and distorting of his tender Body with cords and ropes, to force and fasten it to the whipping stock,

Hail Mary.

10. At the tearing and wounding of his flesh, with the whips,

Hail Mary.

Glory be to the Father, &c.

These Prayers Angelical, &c.

I 3   The

The third Dolorous Mystery.
[Is Crown'd.]

Our Father, &c.
Our Blessed Saviour was exceedingly tormented.

1. At the pressing of the sharp pointed thorns into his sacred Head.
   Hail Mary.
2. At the pulling it off and on, to augment his torments.
   Hail Mary.
3. At his cloathing with Purple, as a counterfeit King.
   Hail Mary.
4. At the holding a Reed in his right hand, as a mock-Scepter.
   Hail Mary.
5. At the scoffing Salutations, Genuflexions, Adorations of the Jews and soldiers.
   Hail Mary.
6. At the spitting in his face.
   Hail Mary.
7. At the smiting his head with the Reed.
   Hail Mary.
8. At the iterated and multiply'd blows, boxes, and buffetings.
   Hail Mary.
9. At his being shew'd to the people

in such a lamentable posture, Behold the Man.

Hail Mary.

16. At the Jews horrid clamors and repeated vociferations, of Away, away with him, crucifie him, crucifie him.

Hail Mary.

Glory be to the Father,&c.

These prayers Angelical,*&c.*

The fourth Dolorous Mystery.
[Carries.]

Our Father,&c.

Our blessed Saviour was exceedingly aggrieved,

1. At the Jews new invented accusation of blasphemy, for making himself the Son of God.

Hail Mary.

2. At the pronunciation of Deaths cruel sentence upon him.

Hail Mary.

3. At his being contumeliously hurried out of *Jerusalem.*

Hail Mary.

4. At his being associated with Thieves, that he might be conceived a complice in their crimes. *Hail Mary.*

5. At the carrying of his own Cross on his shoulders.

Hail Mary.

6. At the oppressing weight of the heavy Cross.

Hail Mary.

7. At the multitude of people thronging about him,

Hail Mary.

8. At the doleful lamentation of the devout women.

Hail Mary.

9. At the compassion of his most sorrowful Mother.

Hail Mary.

10. At the circumstances of the loathsome place, where he was put to death.

Hail Mary.

Glory be to the Father, &c.

These prayers Angelical, &c.

The fifth Dolorous Mystery.

[Is killed.]

Our Father, &c.

Our blessed Saviour was put to excef-

2. At his there standing again naked in the sight of all the Spectators.

Hail Mary.

3. At the boysterous stretching out of his body on the Cross.

Hail Mary.

4. At the piercing of his hands and feet with nails.

Hail Mary.

5. At the Erection of the Cross, with Jesus upon it.

Hail Mary.

6. At the superscription of the Title; of Jesus of Nazareth, King of the Jews.

Hail Mary.

7. At the continued calumnies of the people whilst he hung on the Cross.

Hail Mary.

8. At the sight of his compassionate Mother, standing by his Cross.

Hail Mary.

9. At his vehement thirst upon the Cross.

Hail Mary.

10. At his giving up the Ghost, and expiration on the Cross.

Hail Mary.

Glory be to the Father, &c.

These Prayers Angelical, *&c.*

I believe in God, &c.

To the facred and undivided Trinity, *&c.*

The third Part of the Rofary containing, The five Glo-rious Myfteries.

In the name of the Father, &c.
O Lord open my mouth, *&c.*
I believe in God, &c.

The firft glorious Myftery.
[*Rifes.*]

Our Father, &c.
Our Bleffed Redemer, and his facred
Mother exceedingly rejoyced.

1. At the glory of his Body, now
cloathed with Immortalitie.
Hail Mary.

2. At the joynt Glorification both of
Body and Soul.
Hail Mary.

3. At his exaltation above all Creatures.

Hail Mary.

4. At his entire victory over all his enemies.

Hail Mary.

5. At his delivering the Holy Fathers out of Limbus.

Hail Mary.

6. At the now perfected Redemption of mankind.

Hail Mary.

7. At his being the true cause and perfect exemplar of the future Resurrection of all Mankind.

Hail Mary.

8. At the filling up the places of false Angels.

Hail Mary.

9. At the corroboration, consolation, and confirmation of the Apostles.

Hail Mary.

10. At his frequent Apparitions for forty daies space.

Hail Mary.

Glory be to the Father, &c.

These Prayers Angelical, &c.

The second Glorious Mystery.
[*Ascends.*]

Our Father, &c.

The glorious Virgin-Mother exceedingly rejoiced.

1. At the Ascension of her Son Jesus, in hers, and his Disciples presence.

Hail Mary.

2. At his great Power shewed in his Ascension.

Hail Mary.

3. At the joyful meeting and acclamation of the Angelical spirits.

Hail Mary.

4. At his soaring above all the Heavens.

Hail Mary.

5. At his ascending above the Angelical Quires, and all Creatures whatsoever.

Hail Mary.

6. At his being seated on the right hand of his Eternal Father.

Hail Mary.

7. At his conducting the souls of the Saints with him into heaven.

Hail Mary.

8. At his opening Heaven gates for our entrance.

Hail Mary.

9. At his being appointed the Advocate of Mankind.

Hail Mary.

10. At the great Fruit and Profit redounding to us by his Ascension.

Hail Mary.

Glory be to the Father, &c.
These prayers Angelical, *&c.*

The third Glorious Mystery.
[Sends down.]

Our Father, &c.
The glorious Virgin Mother exceedingly rejoyced,

1. At the miraculous manner of the Holy Ghosts coming.
Hail Mary.
2. At the fulfilling of Chrifts Promise in sending him.
Hail Mary.
3. At the multiplication of tongues, and speaking of all languages.
Hail Mary.
4. At the Apostles confirmation in grace and goodness.
Hail Mary.
5. At their patience, courage and constancy in their persecutions.
Hail Mary.
6. At the confutation of the Jews and Infidels.
Hail Mary.
7. At the sudden multiplication of the faithful.   Hail Mary.

Q   At

8 At the sanctification of Christs Passion.

9. At the great encrease of the divine honour and worship.

Hail Mary.

10. At the accomplishment of the number of the Elect.

Hail Mary.

Glory be to the Father, &c.

These Prayers Angelical, &c.

The fourth glorious Mystery.
[*She Dies.*]

Our Father, &c.

The glorious Virgin-Mothers heart, was replenished with exceeding great joy.

1. At the news of the near approaching dissolution of her soul and body, whereof she was informed by a heavenly messenger.

Hail Mary.

2. At the security of her Glorious and speedy Resurrection.

Hail Mary.

3. At her dying without any dread, terrour, or trouble.

Hail Mary.

4. At the presence of the Apostles at her departure. *Hail Mary.*

5. At the sweet separation of her Soul and Body.

Hail Mary.

6. At the joyful Re-union of her Soul and Body in her Resuscitation and Assumption into Heaven.

Hail Mary.

7. At Christs meeting her accompanied with the Heavenly Citizens.

Hail Mary.

8. At her being exalted above all the Angelical Orders and Hierarchies.

Hail Mary.

9. At her being placed on her Sons right hand. *Hail Mary.*

10. At her being appointed the Advocatrix of mankind.

Hail Mary.

Glory be to the Father, &c.

These Prayers Angelical, &c.

The fifth glorious Mystery.
[Is Crown'd.]

Our Father, &c.

The Blessed Virgins Soul was fill'd with explicable joy.

1. At her being seated upon a Royal throne in the celestial glory.

Hail Mary.

2. At her being cloathed with Royal Garments ; to wit, A Body most pure

and unspotted, and a soul most perfect in all vertue. *Hail Mary.*

3. At her being adorn'd with Royal Jewels; to wit, The plenitude of all prudence, *Science,* and Intelligence in her *Soul*; and of *Clarity, Subtility, Impassibility Agility* in her Body.

Hail Mary.

4. At her being honoured with a royal Ring, to wit, In her *Soul,* (which was the singular Spouse of the eternal King) a singular joy, Glory, and felicity: And in her *Body* (which was singularly instrumental in the eternal Words Incarnation) a singular beauty.

Hail Mary.

5. At her being grac'd with a Royal Scepter; to wit, In her *Soul,* by a special Power which was given her in Heaven and Earth; and in her *Body,* by a special prerogative of glory.

Hail Mary.

6. At her being deck'd with a Royal Crown, out-shining all others in glory, as she excelled all others in vertue.

Hail Mary.

7. At her being crown'd with the silver *Aureola* of Virgins.

Hail Mary.

8. At her being crown'd with the golden *Aureola* of Martyrs.

Hail Mary.

9. At her being crown'd with the Starry *Aureola* of the Doctors.

Hail Mary.

10. At her being crown'd with the verdant, and perpetually florishing *Aureola* of Innocency and Purity.

Hail Mary.

Glory be to the Father, &c.

These Prayers Angelical, &c.

I beleeve in God, &c.

To the sacred and undivided Trinity, &c.

SECTION X.

JESUS:

Or,

The Confraternity of the most sacred Name of Iesus.

IN somuch as there is a pious Fraternity of the most holy *Name of Iesus,* which had its first rise and origin from that of the sacred Rosary (*Et ex illa tanquam ex Matre filia prognata sit*) being (as it were) the Daughter of that Mother ; and to which it is so firmly fastned, & so neerly allied, as that generally (in Catholique Countries) all they who are

are children of the Blessed Mothers Ro-
fary, are also thus members of the *Sons
Society*: It will not be amiss, after this
Declaration of the *Rosary*, to annex a
description of this *Confraternity*; that so
nothing may be wanting, which may
conduce to the devotion of faithful
Christians, and enrich them with spiritual Benefits.

This pious *Confraternity* of the sacred
Name of Jesus, was begun in *Italy*, by
Didacus à Victoria, a Doctor of Divinity, and devout Preacher of S. *Dominicks*
Order, in the year 1564. and soon after
promulgated throughout *Spain*, by *Joannes Micon*, who was another learned
Doctor, and zealous Preacher of the
same Order, the Disciple of that blessed
and famous man, *Ludovicus Bertrandus*.

The Reason and End of the Institution thereof, was to extirpate that exe-
crable (and then Customary) vice of
Swearing by Gods holy Name, and
blaspheming the divine Majesty.

*The Rules of this Confraternity are
these.*

1. They who desire to be of it are
either to have their Names enrolled into a Book provided for that purpose (as
it is said of the *Rosary*:) or to be admitted into this *Confraternity*, (by such as

have power from the Superiours of Saint
Dominicks Order) by some other legal,
lawful, and formal way.

2. Upon the day of our Redeemers
Circumcision (which is the principal,
and indeed the only proper Feast of this
Confraternity,) they are to Confess,
Communicate, and be present at the solemnity then celebrated by their fellow
members of this Confraternity, in the
place appointed by the Chief Director
thereof.

3. Upon the *second Sunday* of each
month, they are to Confess, Communicate and assist at the solemn Mass, and
at the Procession of the Litanies of Jesus, which are then recited in the head
Chappel of the Confraternity.

4. They are with all possible care and
diligence to avoid *swearing* not only in
themselves, but also in all others : admo-
nishing, checking, and correcting (as far
as the Rules of Charity and Discretion
will permit) all such as shall inconside-
rately and rashly Swear, and Blaspheme
in their presence and hearing.

5. They are to assist at the *Anniversary* of their departed Brethren, celebrated upon the first vacant day after the
Feast of the *Circumcision.*

The manner of the Reviving this Rosa-

ry of the holy Name of *JESUS* invented by Joannes Micon, *to implore Chrifts
mercy for our felves* and *for all finners,* is
this.

Taking your Ordinary Bedes of the
Rofary, begin with the fign of the *Crofs,*
 In the Name of the Father, &c.
Then after the recital of one *Pater
Nofter,* Ave Marias and *Creed,* begin
thus,

V. *Intend unto my aid, O God.*
R. *Lord make hafte to help me.*
V. *Glory be to the Father, and to the
Son, and to the Holy Ghoft.*
R. *As it was in the beginnieg, is now
and ever fhall be world without end. Amen.*

The firft part of this Rofary confifts
in the Repetition of thefe words fifty
Times [*O Jefu Chrift, the Son of David,
have mercy upon us*] Meditating during
the recital of each Decade upon one of
the *Five* Myfteries of the *Life* of Our
Bleffed Redeemer *Chrift Jefus,* and ending each Decade with, *Glory be to the
Father, and to the Son, and to the Holy
Ghoft, &c.*

The Myfteries of the firft *Quinqua-
gena* or *Fiftieth.*

1. Chrifts Incarnation,

2. His

2. His Nativity.

3. His Circumcision.

4. His finding in the Temple.

5. His Baptism.

O Iesu Christ the Son of David have mercy upon us.

The second part of this Rosary, consists in the Repetition of these words also fifty times, [*O Iesu of Nazareth King of the Iews, have mercy upon us.*] Meditating in like manner during the recital of each Decade upon one of the *Five* mysteries of the *Death* and *Passion* of our Blessed Redeemer *Christ Iesus,* and ending each Decade with, *Glory be to the Father, &c.* as aforesaid.

The Mysteries of the second *Quinquagena* or *Fiftieth.*

1. Our Saviours washing his Disciples feet.

2. His Prayer in the Garden.

3. His apprehension in the Garden,

4. His carrying of the Cross.

5. His Descent into Hell.

O Iesu of Nazareth, King of the Iews, have mercy upon us.

in the Repetition of thefe words alfo fifty times, [*O Jefu Chrift, Son of the living God, have mercy upon us.*] Meditating likewife during the recital of each Decade upon one of the *Five* Myfteries of the *Glory* of our Bleffed Redeemer Chrift *Jefus,* and ending each Decade with, *Glory be to the Father, and to the Son, and to the holy Ghoft, &c.* as formerly.

The Myfteries of the third *Quinquagena* or *Fiftieth.*

1. Chrifts Refurrection.
2. His Afcenfion.
3. His fending the Holy Ghoft.
4. The Crowning of the Virgin *Mary* and the Saints.
5. The coming to judgement.

O Jefu Chrift Son of the living God, have mercy upon us.

A brief Declaration of the *Crown of our Lord.*

THE devotion call'd the *Crown of our Lord,* Or the *Rofary of the age of Chrift,* or the *Crown of Camaldula,* was invented by one *bleffed Michael,* by birth

Camaldula (a man of admirable piety and sanctity) who chang'd this life for a happy immortality, in the year 1522, since which time this prayer hath been far and near propagated throughout the whole world, with the Churches general applause and approbation, and to the great profit and comfort of all faithful Christians.

The Tenor of the Brief of Pope *Leo* the tenth, (as far forth as it concerns the confirmation, and declares the form of reciting this sacred Crown) is as here follows.

Bishop Leo *the servant of Gods servants, to all and singular the faithful people of Christ, to whom these his letters shall come, sends greeting, and the Apostolical Benediction.*

We have lately had notice from persons worthy of belief, that a certain *ancient Hermit, of the sacred wilderness of Camaldula* having already finish'd fifteen years of his earthly Pilgrimage in great austerity, as a Recluse shut up within the narrow limits of one only Cell: Hath conceiv'd by divine inspiration, as may be piously believ'd from whence every right thought proceeds) that it would much redound to the honour of Christ our Lord and Saviour, and conduce to

the encrease of devotion in the hearts
of all pious Christians: If as [according
to the very ancient institution, and generally receiv'd custome] several godly
people use to recite *sixty three Angelical
Salutations, with our Lords Prayer seven times interpos'd*, in honour of the
most blessed Virgin *Mary*, according to
the number of years which she is esteemed to have liv'd upon earth, which kind
of prayer is call'd *the Virgins Crown*, so
they would also inure themselves to recite *thirty three Lords Prayers, interpo-
sing four Angelical Salutations* in the honour of our Redeemer, for a commemoration of the years, in which he convers'd upon earth amongst men, which
would be [as it were] *our Lords Crown*,
&c.

We whom it behoves to promote the
honour of our Lord *Iesus Christ* as far
forth as he shall enable us, and to add
fewel to the devotion of his faithful
flock; *Do approve and confirm* the aforesaid manner of Prayer, invented by that
ancient and recluded Hermit, and will
have it call'd *the Crown of our Lord*, &c.
Given at *Florence* the 18. of *February*, in
the year, 1516.

The same Rosary or Crown of our
Lord, was afterwards confirm'd by Pope

Gregory the 13.and endow'd with more
and greater Indulgences: *vide Augusti-*
num Florentinum, Lucam Eremitam,
Bucelinum in Annalibus Benedictinis,&c.

The *Crown* therefore confisting of 33.
Pater Nosters, or *Lords Prayers* [con-
fonant to the number of years,in which
our dear Redeemer convers'd with men
in his humane flesh upon earth, to merit
for us a happy Crown of Glory in Hea-
ven]and of four *Ave Maries* or Angelical Salutations, with *one Creed* added
for a conclusion, is divided into *four*
parts [whereof the *three first* parts are
Decades or *Tens,* there being in each of
them a *ten-times-repeated Lords Prayer,*
and one *Angelical Salutation:* and in
the *fourth* part there is only a *Thrice-re-*
peated Lords Prayer, with one Angelical Salutation and the Creed] and may
be recited as it is here distinctly set
down, with an additional point of *Me-*
ditation upon some of the pious Mysteries of our Saviours life, and a short
Aspiration, which may easily be dilated
with more affections and resolutions according to each ones Spirit of devotion.

The

The firft part of the Crown of our Lord.

Of Chrifts coming into the World.

I.

OUr dear Redeemer defcended from his royal Throne, from his eternal Fathers Bofom, from his happy heaven into this vale of mifery, and cloath'd himfelf with humane flefh in the holy Virgins womb.

O *Iefu* ! how exceffive is your Mercy, how infinite your affection, how ftupendious your condefcendency to undeferving man ? Ah ! that my heart were perfectly free from all that difpleafeth you, that fo it might deferve perpetually to harbour you.

Our Father, &c.

2.

HE [being conceiv'd] infpir'd his facred Virgin Mother to take a journey into the mountains of *Iudea*, there to vifit, falute, and ferve St. *Elizabeth* her Kinfwoman.

O *Iefu* ! that my foul were always pliable, docible, obedient to correfpond to your fweet and facred impulfes, moti-

ons and aspirations ! how cheerfully
should I then serve your soveraign Majesty, and how charitably should I assist
my necessitous neighbour.

Our Fathers &c.

3.

AFter he had been carried nine
moneths in his mothers chast entrails, he was born in a cold stable,
wrapp'd in poor rags, cradled in a hard
cribb.

O *Iesu* ! make me in love with poverty, humility, and mortification, which
you have made so amiable by practising
them in your own divine person.

Our Father, &c.

4.

THe Angels congratulate his happy
birth with their heavenly Canticles,
and the shepherds humbly, joyfully, and
admiringly adore him.

O *Iesu* ! let my tongue incessantly sing
forth your Praises, let my heart perpetually breath forth acts of gratitude for
your Mercies, and let my soul sweetly
melt away in her reciprocal affections.

Our Father, &c.

5. He

5.

UPon the eighth day after his Nativity, he was circumcis'd and called *Jefus*.

O *Jefu*! O facred and fugred Name! O *Jefu*, be unto me a *Iefus* ! O that my tongue, heart, and hands, with all my fenfes, powers and faculties of body and foul, were truly circumcis'd from all fuperfluous, curious, vitious inclinations, paffions, and affections, that fo I might never more think, fpeak, or act any thing offenfive to your divine will and liking.

Our *Father*, &c.

6.

HE was diligently fought out by the Eaftern Sages, humbly ador'd by them, and highly honoured by their royal Prefents and Oblations.

O *Iefu* ! let me never leave feeking till I find you, the only belov'd Object of all my affections, and ftrengthen me [*fweet Iefu* !] to make a total Oblation, Confecration, and Refignation of my whole felf to your holy will and pleafure, entirely, irrevocably, eternally.

Our *Father*, &c.

7.

HE was carried to the Temple in his sacred Mothers arms, to be presented as her first-born to his eternal Father, shewing himself in all things subject to the Law.

O *Iesu* ! shall not I humble my self, and submit to all men for your sake ?

Our Father, &c.

8.

HE to avoid *Herods* cruelty, sustain'd a tedious banishment in his tender years.

O *Iesu* ! give me patience in all my persecutions, temptations and troubles, and let not my grievous sins banish me from your sweet grace and presence.

Our Father, &c.

9.

HE return'd from *Egypt* after his seven years sufferings.

O *Iesu* ! let your efficacious grace recall me from vice to vertue : let me return into you my first Origin, and let me repose in you my only center and security.

Our Father, &c.

10. He

10.

HE dwelt with his Parents in the City *Nazareth.*

O *Iesu!* dwell in my soul *here* by your grace, that my soul may dwell with you *hereafter* in your eternal glory.

Our Father.

O Sacred *Virgin-Mother!* who having conceiv'd your divine Son without sin, and brought him forth without sorrow, serv'd him so diligently during the time of his minority: appease him (I beseech you) in my behalf, by your powerful Prayers and intercession. *Hail Mary.*

The second Part.

Of Christs conversation amongst men.

1.

OUr dear Redeemer, being twelve years old, went up with his Parents to *Ierusalem,* to perform his devotions, where he was lost, sought, and after three days found in the temple.

O *Iesu!* replenish my heart with solid devotion, that sincerely seeking you, I may happily find you, and having found you, I may faithfully keep you.

come.

company in my interiour for evermore.
Our Father, &c.

2.

HE return'd with his Parents to *Na-zareth*, and was subject unto them.

O *Iesu* I break my rebellious will, that I may promptly obey you and my Superiours, according to your most perfect example.

Our Father, &c.

3.

HE being thirty years old was baptized by St. *Iohn* in the river *Iordan.*

O *Iesu* permit not my sinful soul to pass forth of my body, till it be baptiz'd in a river of tears, and restor'd to purity by the Sacrament of Penance.

Our Father, &c.

4.

HE fasted forty days and nights in the Desert, and was tempted by the Devil.

O *Iesu* I give me courage to subdue all sensuality, constancy to resist all temptations, and strength to conquer all my enemies.

Our Father, &c.

5. He

5.

HE painfully went from place to place, preaching the Gospel to the people.

O *Iesu* ! let my soul incessantly thirst after your honour, and the salvation of my neighbour.

Our Father, &c.

6.

HE honoured marriage with his presence, and with his first miracle, and afterwards (for three years space) he plentifully pour'd forth his miraculous benefits upon all sorts of Persons.

O *Iesu*, overflow my heart with a general affection and compassion towards all Christians; and permit me not to grow weary in performing works of piety.

Our Father, &c.

7.

HE oftentimes spent whole nights in Prayer, and suffered hunger, thirst, cold, heat, poverty, and persecution for

8.

HIs chief leſſon was humility: *Learn of me, for I am meek, and humble of heart.*

O *Jeſu!* This is one of the vertues I chiefly ſtand in need of; Ah! that my heart were truly ſimple, ſupple, innocent, and humble! how happy a ſcholler ſhould I be (*O my Redeemer!*) in your holy School, could I as cheerfully pra-ctiſe, as I can eaſily reſolve?

Our Father, &c.

9.

HIs principal precept was Charity, *I give you a new commandment, that ye love one another.*

O *Ieſu!* this is the other vertue I principally want and wiſh for; Ah! that my whole interiour and exteriour, my heart, ſoul, body, and ſenſes, were no-thing but pure *Charity!* that ſo it might be impoſſible for me to ſpeak, think, act, or breath any thing but the perfect love of you and my neighbour.

Our Father, &c.

tears amidst the peoples applauses and acclamations.

O *Jesu!* give me a true sight of my self, and of the World, that perfectly knowing my own vility and its vanity, I may incessantly bewail my self-wretchedness, weep for the worlds wickedness, and render to you only all honour and glory.

Our Father, &c.

O Sacred *Virgin-Mother!* who so faithfully, diligently, and devoutly accompany'd, follow'd, and serv'd your divine Son in his manly age : appease him (I beseech you) in my behalf, by your powerful prayers and intercession.

Hail Mary, &c.

The third part.

Of *Christs bitter Death and Passion.*

1.

Our dear Redeemer, after his last supper, washed the feet of his Disciples, and instituted the Sacrament of the Eucharist.

O *Jesu!* which shall I most admire, your stupendious humilitie? or your unheard-off charitie?

Our Father, &c: H₂

2.

HE entred the Garden with his Disciples, where after he had most fervently prayed, he fell into a vehement Agony, in which, bloud mixed with sweat, trickled down from his whole body.

O *Jesu!* how great are my sins, which are the cause of your so great sorrow? place your Passion [I beseech you] between them and your judgment; O let your sufferings cancel their heynousness, and let your precious bloud wash away their erronious filthiness.

Our Father, &c.

3.

HE was seized on by a crew of armed Souldiers, manacled with cords, dragged away to *Annas* and *Caiphas.*

O *Jesu!* dissolve the bands of my unruly passions, perverse inclinations, and impure affections, and take me, tie me, shackle me, and draw me unto you with the sweet cords of your sacred love and charity.

Our Father, &c.

4.

IN the whole night of his Passion, he suffered all sorts of injuries, vexations, and torments.

O *Iesu!* and shall I repine at small pains and persecutions ? shall I faint under the light burthen which your loving hand lays upon my shoulders ? O meek lamb of God ! pardon my past impatience, and give me a perseverant Resignation to your will and pleasure.

Our Father, &c.

5.

HE was contemptibly hurried away to *Pilate* and *Herod,* and by them scorn'd as a silly Ideot.

O *Iesu!* you are every way humbled, depressed, annihilated, and I seek nothing but honour, applause, estimation ! Is this to imitate you, my Lord and Master ? O change me, correct me, convert me, by your power, in your mercy, by your example.

Our Father, &c.

6.

HIs tender body was ty'd naked to a pillar, and torn with whips and scourges.

O *Jesu* I uncloath me of the old man, ith all his wicked works, and reveft e with the new, created in juftice and ſctity, according to your own heart.

Our *Father*, &c.

7.

HE was beaten with a cane, buffeted with their fifts, fpurned with their ſeet, defil'd with their fpittle, crown'd vith thorns, every way abuſed.

O *Jesu* I the beauty of men and Angels I how are you worried for my wickedneſs? O wound my foul with a deep fenſe of your fufferings, that I may henceforth abſolutely deteft all fin, trample upon all fenſuality, cancel all vanity, ferve you more innocently, and adhere to you more fervently.

Our *Father*, &c.

8.

HE was forc'd to carry his heavy Croſs upon his weak and wounded fhoulders from *Jerufalem* to mount *Calvary*.

O *Jesu*! let me cheerfully take up the Croſs of ſelf-contempt, ſelf-abnegation, ſelf-denial, and follow you till death, conftantly, couragiouſly, perſeverantly.

Our *Father*, &c.

He

9.

HE was stripp'd naked, and stretch'd on the Cross, having his hands and feet barbarously nayl'd unto it, and his side pierc'd with a Launce.

O *Iefu!* strip me of all that displeases the eyes of your divine Majefty, dilate my heart with celeftial affections, and fasten my soul to your felf, with the sweet nails of your sacred Love.

Our Father, &c.

10.

HAving hung three hours on the Cross, inclining his head, he gave up the Ghoft.

O *Iefu!* you died for me, that I might live eternally: O let me die to all things, that I may henceforth live to you only, who are to me *All in All.*

Our Father, &c.

O Sacred *Virgin Mother!* who so patiently, conftantly, perfeverantly stood by your divine Son, dying on the Cross for me; appeafe him (I befeech you) in my behalf, by your powerful Prayers and Interceffion.

Hail Mary, &c.

The

The fourth Part.

Of Christs glorious Triumph after Death.

1.

OUr dear Redeemer, rising victori-
ously (upon the third day) from
his Sepulcher, replenished the hearts of
his holy Mother, Disciples and Friends,
with unspeakable joy and gladness.

O *Iesu* I give me grace, strength, and
courage to shake off the death of my in-
veterate vices and bad customs, and to
rise to newness of life and conversation.
O let me henceforth savour the things
which are above, and not these vain, vile,
terrene, and transitory trifles, which can
never satiate my soul, created for you
only.   *Our Father, &c.*

2.

HE triumphantly ascended to heaven
(on the fourth day after his resurrection) amidst the jubilee of Angels,
in the company of the Patriarks, in the
sight of his sacred Mother, Disciples, and
Friends, where he sits at his Fathers
right hand, blessed for evermore.

O

O *Iesu* ! that my soul might follow you, the only object of her affections ! O that I could incessantly aspire to you, long after you, languish for you, my only center and security, the only comfort of my life, and Crown of all my desires.

'   *Our Father, &c.*

3.

HE sent down his holy Spirit upon his Apostles, and the rest of his chosen children to instruct them in his will, to encourage them in their duties, to confirm them in their Faith, to assist them in their preaching, to strengthen them in their persecutions.

'   O *Iesu* ! send also your holy Spirit to cure, cleanse, and comfort my sick, sinful and sad soul, adorn each corner of my interiour with your divine love and grace, that your sacred Spirit may find there a sweet and grateful habitation ; rule, reign, and remain in my heart (O *Iesu* ! *King of Glory* !) for evermore.

'   *Our Father, &c.*

O *Sacred Virgin-Mother* ! whose soul was dilated with such unspeakable joy and sweetness in the glorious Resurrection and admirable Ascention of your divine Son, JESUS : appease him (I be-

feech you) in my behalf, by your powerful Prayers and Interceffion.

Hail Mary, &c.

Conclude this holy Crown with the
Apoftles Creed.

I believe in God, &c.

*Thirty three Elevations and Petitions
to Iefus our bleffed Redeemer, in honour of the thirty three years of his
holy Life.*

1. O Good Jefu, the Word of the Father! convert us.
2. O good Jefu, the lamb of God! purifie us.
3. O Good Jefu, our Mafter! teach us.
4. O good Jefu, the Prince of Peace!
govern us.
5. O good Jefu, the fure hope of penitent finners! behold us.
6. O good Jefu, our Refuge! defend us.
7. O good Jefu, our Inftructor! direct
us.
8. O good Jefu, our Patience! comfort
us.
9. O good Jefu, the chief Comforter of
fad Souls! refresh us.
10. O good Jefu, our Redeemer! fave

11. O good Jesu, our Lord and our God I possess us.

12. O good Jesu, the life, the way, and the truth I enliven us.

13. O good Jesu, our firm foundation I strengthen us.

14. O good Jesu, the light of the world I illuminate me.

15. O good Jesu, the pattern of all vertues! perfect us.

16. O good Jesu, our Mediator I sanctifie us.

17. O good Jesu, the Physician of our souls! heal us.

18. O good Jesu, our Judge I absolve us.

19. O good Jesu, the Sun of Justice! shine upon us.

20. O good Jesu, our King I deliver us.

21. O good Jesu, Son of *David!* pity us.

22. O good Jesu, our sanctification I justifie us.

23. O good Jesu, the living bread descending from heaven I satiate us.

24. O good Jesu, the wine bringing forth Virgins I inebriate us.

25. O good Jesu, our loving Father! bless us.

26. O good Jesu, the only joy of our hearts! visit us.

27. O good Jesu, our soveraign helper! assist us.

28. O good Jesu, the mirrour of purity! cleanse us.

29. O good Jesu, our faithful Lover! transform us.

30. O good Jesu, the Propitiation for our sins! hide us in your wounds.

31. O good Jesu, the painful Shepherd! feed us.

32. O good Jesu, the eternal Life! receive us into the number of your Elect.

33. O good Jesu, the crown and glory of all Saints! bring us to your heavenly kingdom.

Give unto us, we most humbly beseech you, O gracious Lord Jesu! what is best pleasing to your divine Majesty: behold we wholly abandon our selves, and all that concerns us into your most holy hands: Dispose of us as you please, and direct us all to accomplish your blessed will, and to submit to your sacred disposition for time and eternity.

Litania in honorem Iesu Christi Domini nostri quæ in Processione Domi-
nica 2ᵉ cujusque mensis recitantur,
in Capella S. Rosarii.

K Trie eleison.
  Christe eleison.
Kyrie eleison.
Iesu audi nos.
Iesu exaudi nos.
Pater de cœlis Deus,
Fili Redemptor mundi Deus,
Spiritus Sancte Deus,
Sancta Trinitas unus Deus,
Iesu! fili Dei vivi,
Iesu! splendor Patris,
Iesu! candor lucis æterna,
Iesu! Rex gloriæ,
Iesu! Sol justitiæ,
Iesu! fili Mariæ Virginis,
Iesu! admirabilis,
Iesu! Deus fortis,
Iesu! Pater futuri sæculi,
Iesu! magni consilii Angele,
Iesu! potentissime,
Iesu! patientissime,

Miserere nobis.

The Litanies of our Lord Iesus, which are recited in the Procession, made on the second Sunday of each month, in the Chappel of the holy Rosary, according to the third Rule of the Confraternity of the Name of Iesus.

Lord have mercy upon us,
Christ have mercy upon us,
Lord have mercy upon us.
O Iesu! hear us.
O Iesu! mercifully hear us.
God the Father of Heaven,
God the Son, Redeemer of the world,
God the Holy Ghost,
O holy Trinity, one God,
O Iesu! Son of the living God,
O Iesu! splendor of the Father,
O Iesu! candor of eternal light,
O Iesu! King of glory,
O Iesu! Sun of justice,
O Iesu! Son of the Virgin *Mary*,
O Iesu! most admirable,
O Iesu! the strong God,
O Iesu! Father of the future world,
O Iesu! the Angel of great counsel,
O Iesu! most powerful,
O Iesu! most patient,

Have mercy upon us.

Iesu! obedientissime,
Iesu! mitis & humilis corde,
Iesu! amator castitatis,
Iesu! exemplar virtutum,
Iesu! zelator animarum,
Iesu! refugium nostrum,
Iesu! Pater pauperum,
Iesu! thesaurus fidelium,
Iesu! bone pastor,
Iesu! lux vera,
Iesu! sapientia eterna,
Iesu! bonitas infinita,
Iesu! via, veritas, & vita,
Iesu! gaudium Angelorum,
Iesu! Magister Apostolorum,
Iesu! Doctor, Evangelistorum,
Iesu! fortitudo Martyrum,
Iesu! lumen Confessorum,
Iesu! puritas Virginum,
Iesu! corona Sanctorum omnium.

Miserere nobis.

    Propitius esto,
      Parce nobis Iesu!
    Propitius esto,
      Exaudi nos Iesu!

Ab omni peccato,
Ab ira tua,
Ab insidiis Diaboli,
A spiritu fornicationis,
A morte perpetua,
A neglectu inspirationum tuarum,

Libera nos Iesu!

D

O Jesu! most obedient,
O Jesu! meek and humble hearted,
O Jesu! the lover of chastity,
O Jesu! the exemplar of vertues,
O Jesu! the zealer of souls,
O Jesu! our refuge,
O Jesu! the Father of the poor,
O Jesu! the treasure of the faithful,
O Jesu! the good Shepherd,
O Jesu! the true light,
O Jesu! the eternal Wisdom,
O Jesu! infinite goodness,
O Jesu! the way, the truth, & the life,
O Jesu! the joy of the Angels,
O Jesu! the Master of the Apostles,
O Jesu! the teacher of the Evangelists,
O Jesu! the strength of the Martyrs,
O Jesu! the light of the Confessors,
O Jesu! the purity of Virgins,
O Jesu! the crown of all Saints,

Have mercy upon us.

Be propitious unto us,
   And spare us, O Jesu!
Be propitious unto us,
   And hear us, O Jesu!

From all sin,
From your anger,
From the deceits of the Devil,
From the spirit of fornication,
From eternal death,
From a neglect of your inspirations,

Deliver us, O Jesus!

By

Per mysteriū sacta Incarnationis tuæ,
Per Nativitatem tuam,
Per divinissimam vitam tuam,
Per labores tuos,
Per Agoniam & Passionem tuam.
Per Crucem & derelictionem tuam,
Per mortem & sepulturam tuam,
Per Resurrectionē & Ascensionē tuā,
Per gaudia & gloriam tuam.

Libera nos Jesu.

Agnus Dei, qui tollis peccata mundi,
  Parce nobis Iesu!
Agnus Dei, qui tollis peccata mundi,
  Exaudi nos Iesu!
Agnus Dei qui tollis peccata mundi,
  Miserere nobis Iesu!
Iesu audi nos. Iesu exaudi nos.

Oremus.

DOmine Iesu Christe, qui dixisti, Peti-
te & accipietis, quærite & invenie-
tis, pulsate & aperietur vobis; concede qua-
sumus nobis humilimè petentibus, ut te toto corde, tota anima, tota virtute diliga-
mus, & a tui nominis laude nunquam ces-
semus. Amen.

  Verse. Exaudiat nos Dominus Iesus
Christus.

  Resp. Amen.

  Et benedictio Dei Omnipotentis, Patris & Filii, & Spiritus Sancti, descendat
super nos & maneat semper. Amen.

By the myſtery of your Incarnation, ⎫
By your Nativity, ⎪
By your moſt divine life, ⎪
By your labours upon earth, ⎪
By your bloudy Agonie and Paſſion, ⎬ Deliver us, O Ieſu!
By your Croſs and dereliction, ⎪
By your Death and Burial, ⎪
By your Reſurrection & Aſcenſion, ⎪
By your Joys and your Glory. ⎭

Lamb of God who takeſt away the
fins of the world,

Spare us, O Jeſu!

Lamb of God, who takeſt away the
fins of the world,

Hear us, O Jeſu!

Lamb of God, who takeſt away the
fins of the world.

Have mercy upon us, O Jeſu!

O Jeſu, hear us. O Jeſu, mercifully
hear us.

Let us pray.

O Lord Jeſu Chriſt, who haſt ſaid,
Ask and ye ſhall have, ſeek and ye
ſhall find, knock and it ſhall be opened
unto you : Grant unto us what we here
moſt humbly beg of your ſacred Majeſty, that we may love you with our
whole heart, ſoul, and ſtrength, and never
ceaſe from intoning the praiſes of your
holy name. *Amen.*

Ver. Our Lord Jeſus Chriſt graciouſ-
ly hear us. &c   M   Sect.

SECTION XI.

MARIA,

OR,

The Devotion called, The Bondage *of the blessed Virgin* Mary.

1. *The Author, and Origin, of the Bondage.*

THis Devotion of the *Bondage* of the Blessed Virgin, so much practised in these our daies, throughout all *Spain* (saies Father *Anthony Tepes*) had its beginning in *Hungary* about the year 1010. by the means of St. *Gerard* a glorious Monk and Martyr of St. *Bennets* Order, the Apostle of that Countrey, and Bishop of *Chanadin,* which is a City in the Confines of *Moravia* and *Hungarie.* By whose Counsel and advice, (saies *Baronius;*) the most holy

King *Stephen* gave himself, and his whole
Kingdom by Vow and Oblation, to the
sacred Virgin Mother: And the *Hunga-
rian* Church (saies Bishop *Cartuitius*,)
did so highly honour this Blessed Virgin; that they celebrate the feast of her
glorious *Assumption*, (which in their
language they call by excellency *Diem
Dominæ*, the Ladies day) with an
equal Solemnitie to that of *Christmas*
and *Easter*; and style themselves, *The
Blessed Virgins Bondslaves.*

    2. *An ancient and Authentique Ex-
    ample of the practice of this Bon-
    dage.*

SOon after St. *Gerard*, lived our St. *Peter Damian* (the learned Cardinal
and Bishop of *Ostia*;) who gives us at
large, a rare example of this *Bondage*, in
his brother *Marinus* (a devout servant
of the Blessed Virgin;) in these words:
  Marinus (the brother of *Peter Damian*) whilst he yet flourished with
strength and health; unclothing himself of his garments, and putting about
his neck the Belt wherewith he was gir-
ded; delivered up himself to the sacred
Virgin before her Altar, as a *servil Bonds-
slave,*

flave, and treating himfelf as fuch a one, whipped himfelf in the fame place before her, faying ; *O my glorious Lady, the Myrrour of Virginal Purity, and perfect Pattern of all Vertues ! &c.* Behold now *I give my felf to you as a fervant, fubmitting the neck of my proftrate heart, to the Empire of your power. Bow me, mollifie me, receive me ; and let not your Piety defpife me a finner, whofe Immaculate Virginity brought forth the Author of all Sanctity. By this fmall gift, I offer you the Tribute of my fervitude and Bondage ; and henceforth, fo long as I fhall live, I promife to pay unto you this yearly Revenue.*

And fo laying a certain fum of *money*, *in Altaris trepidine*, upon the *corner of the Altar* ; he departed with a firm confidence to find the mercy, which he had faithfully fought, and humbly implored.

This holy Man continuing this Devotion during his *life-time*, deferved to be particularly vifited and comforted by the Bleffed Virgin, *at the hour of his death* : To whom he fpake in this fort : *Whence is it (O Soveraign Lady, Queen of Heaven and Earth !) that you thus vouchfafe to give a vifit to your unworthy Bondflave ? Beftow on me your Bleffing,*

(O

(*O my Lady!*) *and permit me not to go into darkness, whom you have been graciously pleased to visit with the light of your glorious presence.*

Then turning towards the by-standers: *The Queen of the World was here,* (saies he) *the Mother of the Eternal Monarch was present: She hath shewed me the gladness of her countenance, given me her holy blessing, and is hence returned into heaven.*

And soon after his departing Soul followed his sacred Mistris: leaving a most lively and memorable example, to excite posterity to the like piety and devotion.

3. *Whereupon this Devotion of the Bondage is grounded.*

THis Devotion of Bondage, is chiefly grounded upon that most heroique Act of Humilitie, which the sacred Virgin produced at the time of our Saviours Incarnation: when being declared Gods Mother by the Angelical Messenger, she answered: *Behold the Handmaid of our Lord* : Luk.1.38.

Whereby she depressing her self into the center of her own nothing, chose undoubtedly the meanest degree of servitude and Bondage to the divine Majestie, upon contemplation that his Infinite Greatness should so humble it self, as to become Man in her womb for the worlds Redemption.

And surely if we will only put together the several sentences of sacred Writ which expresly concern her; we shall find, that she made up the *Chain* of her *Bondage* with the links of twelve most excellent vertues.

1. Virginal MODESTY, *She was troubled at the Angels word.* Luk. 1. 29.

2. Mature PRUDENCE. *She cast in her mind, what manner of Salutation this should be?* Luk. 1. 29.

3. Bashfull TIMEROUSNES. *Fear not* MARY, *for thou hast found grace with God.* Luk. 1. 30.

4. Immaculate CHASTITY. *How shall this be, seeing I know not man?* Luk. 1. 34.

5. Profound HUMILITIE. *Behold the Handmaid of our Lord.* Luk. 1. 38.

6. Perfect OBEDIENCE. *Be it done to me, according to thy word.* Luk. 1. 38.

7. Firm FAITH. *Blessed art thou*

who haft believed. Luk.1.45.

8. Grateful THANKSGIVING. *My Soul doth Magnifie our Lord.* Luk.1.46.

9. True POVERTY. *She wrapped the Infant in fwadling cloathes and laid him in a manger.* Luk.2.7.

10. Invincible PATIENCE. *Thy Father and I, grieving have fought thee.* Luk.1.48.

11. Charitable PIETIE, *Son, they have no Wine.* John 2.3.

12. Perfeverant CONSTANCY. *Near to the Crofs of Jefus, ftood his Mother.* John 19.25.

In imitation therefore of thefe her holy vertues, and efpecially of that high *Act of Humility* (as is aforefaid) by which fhe rendring her felf Gods *Bond-flave*, was raifed to be his *Mother*: (for no fooner had She finifhed that humble fpeech, *Behold the handmaid of our Lord, be it unto me according to thy faying,* but *the Word was made Flefh, and dwelt in her* facred bowels.)

As alfo, in confideration of the Soveraign Dominion, which God hath given her in Heaven over the Angels: (*The Queen ftood at thy right hand.* Pfal.44.) on Earth over men, (*Kings reign by me, &c,* Prov. 18.) *And thou alone haft overcome all herefies in the whole world,* fings the Church;) And over Hell, and the Devill; (*She fhall bruife thy head,* Gen. 3.). And Laftly, in remembrance that Chrift *Jefus* our Redeemer, was himfelf fubject and obedient unto her, *Luk.* 3. 51.

In Imitation, Confideration, and Memory of thefe things (I fay) this holy manner of honouring the moft facred Virgin, was (as you have briefly heard) invented above fix hundred years fince, (by divine infpiration as we may pioufly believe) and is much practifed amongft the devouter fort of Chriftians throughout the world, even at this day.

4. *The Rules of this Devotion of the Bondage.*

1. IN fign of the Invifible and fpiritual Chain, which links our fincere affection to the facred Virgin, and moves us to become her fervants and Bondflaves, we muft wear fome little material *Chain* or manacle of Iron, about our middle, neck, or arms.

2. We are to have the *Chain* we intend to wear, bleffed by fome Prieft, in

The Blessing of the Chains.

Verf. A*Djutorium nostrum in nomine* Domini.

Resp. *Qui fecit cœlum & terram.*

Verf. *Sit Nomen Domini Benedictum.*

Resp. *Ex hoc, nunc, & usque in saeculum.*

Verf. *Domine exaudi orationem meam.*

Resp. *Et clamor meus at te veniat.*

Verf. *Dominus vobiscum.*

Resp. *Et cum Spiritu tuo.*

Oremus.

O*Mnipotens sempitern: Deus, qui vincula peccatorum nostrorum disrumpis, ut libertate Filiorum gaudere valeamus; & qui ad vincula salutis, hominem advocas, dicens: Injice pedem tuum in compedes illius, & ne acedieris vinculis ejus; Hæc vincula que in signum perpetuæ servitutis, ad honorem Beatæ Virginis, servi ejus deferre intendunt, Bene † dicere, & Sancti † ficare digneris: Et concede eis, sic devote illa gerere, ut vivendo, candore castitatis illustrentur, ac moriendo, a vinculis peccatorum absoluti, intercessione ejusdem sanctissima Matris Maria tecum & cum illa in regno gloria congaudere* *valeant fine fine. Qui vivis & regnas in fecula faculorum. Amen.*

Then he fprinkles the chains with holy water faying,

† *In nomine Patris, & Filii,* † *& Spiritus Sancti, Amen.*

3. We may do well to make choice of fome day, dedicated to the Virgins honour, for the entring into this *Bondage,* and putting on of this *Chain* to make our Profeffion more memorable and folemn.

Note that the moft proper and principal Feafts of this *Bondage,* are the *Annunciation,* and the *Affumption:* The firft, being the Origin thereof grounded upon thofe words of the facred Virgin to the Angel ; *Behold the Handmaid of our Lord:* And the fecond, being her taking poffeffion of that fovereign Dominion, next after God, whereupon the whole duty of this devout fervitude depends. In thefe daies therefore, we are more particularly and zealoufly to er and Oblation made at our first entrance into it; as it shall be hereafter set down.

4. We should also prepare our selves before hand, by some particular Devotion; as Fasting, Mortification, Meditation, Almes-deeds, Confession; Communion; to render the Profession of our Bondage more efficacious and meritorious.

5. Then at the time appointed; we are to kneel down reverently before some Altar or Image of our Blessed Lady, and make an Oblation of our selves unto her, in manner following.

The Prayer and Oblation of our selves in Bondage to the Blessed Virgin.

O Blessed *Mary*, Mother of God, Queen of Heaven, and Empress of the whole Universe! Behold I *N. N.* a most unworthy wretch, humbly prostrate before the Throne of your Mercy and Goodness, heartily Congratulating your glory and greatness, and faithfully acknowledging your soveraign Power, and Dominion (next after God) over my self and all Creatures : Do here make a voluntary, absolute, and irrevocable Oblation, Donation, and consecration of my self unto your Majesty; desiring, intending and resolving to be hereafter, not only your loyal subject and servant, but even your real vassal and Bond-slave. In confirmation whereof, I will continually wear this material *Chain* about my Body, both as a Badge of my now professed Bondage, and also as a token of my perpetual affection towards you.

Vouchsafe therefore, O Soveraign Queen! to Receive, Admit, and own me henceforth, as a thing peculiarly yours; and as such a one, to defend and protect me, during this life, from the snares of sin; to dissipate and break asunder, at the hour of my death, the shackles of Satan; and to draw my departing soul, by this happy *Chain*, to your Sons heavenly Kingdom; there to praise, admire, and enjoy, both him and you for all eternity. *Amen.*

6. After the recital of this oblation of your self in Bondage to the Blessed Virgin; put the chain about some part of your body, and endeavour thenceforward, to walk worthy so noble a Profession.

The

5. *The Practises and Exercises of this Devotion of the Bondage.*

1. The *first Exercise* may consist of jaculatory Prayers, frequently darting out these or the like affections.

O my blessed Lady! I am your servant, and the Bond-slave of your greatness.

Or, *O my Lord Jesu! I am yours, and your Mothers Servant and Bond-slave.*

Or, *Holy* Mary, *Mother of God! pray for us sinners (and your bond-slaves) now, and in the hour of our Death.*

Or when you hear the clock strike, salute the blessed Virgin with an *Ave Maria,* to which all Christians are invited by Pope *Leo* the tenth, and *Paul* the fifth, who gave large Indulgences thereunto.

Or, say then, *blessed be the hour and day in which our Lord Jesus Christ was born of the Virgin Mary.*

Or, *Eternity is at hand.*

Or, *Jesus, Maria, Joseph.*

Or, *let the Souls of the faithful departed, rest in Peace.*

2. The *second Exercise* may be a short pair of Bedes, consisting of *three Paters,* in honour of the holy Trinity, and *twelve*

Aves, in honour of the twelve Priviledges of the sacred Virgin, to be said in manner following.

1. *Pater Noster, &c.*

Thanking the eternal Father for having made choice of so worthy a daughter.

1. *Ave Mary,* &c. considering her eternal Predestination.
2. *Ave,* her immaculate Conception.
3. *Ave,* her most pure Virginity.
4. *Ave,* her most admirable Maternity.

2. *Pater Noster, &c.*

Thanking the eternal Son, for having made choyce of so worthy a Mother.

1. *Ave,* considering her most happy Child-birth.
2. *Ave,* her soveraign Dominion, not only over the world, but over the Creator of the world : [*He was subject to them,* Luke 2.
3. *Ave,* her excellent Purity of Soul and Body.
4. *Ave,* her continual and sublime Contemplation.

3. *Pater*

3. *Pater Noster, &c.*

Thanking the Holy Ghost, for having made choice of so worthy a Spouse.

1. *Ave,* considering her sweet departure out of this life.

2. *Ave,* her miraculous Resuscitation.

3. *Ave,* her glorious Assumption.

4. *Ave,* her eternal Glorification and Coronation.

3. The *third Exercise* may be a crown consisting of *five* pretious Pearls, in honour of the blessed Virgins *five principal Vertues,* to be offer'd up to her in the manner following.

1. *The Iasper of Faith:* Produce Acts of *Faith* with most ardent affection: saying, *O Soveraign Queen, I firmly believe that you were an entire Virgin, both before and after your happy Child-birth: That you are the true mother of Gods Son; That your life was without the least Sin: That you were a Martyr at the foot of the Cross: That you are exalted above all pure Creatures in the Celestial glory: That you are our Advocate, interceding for us wretched sinners, &c.*

Add such other points of *Faith* as

your devotion shall suggest, and then conclude thus.

Receive [most sacred Lady] this Protestation of my Faith, as a Iasper-stone belonging to your Crown, and obtain for me a lively, perfect, and perseverant Faith unto the end. Amen.

And recite one *Ave Mary* to this intention.

2. *The Emerald of Hope :* Produce Acts of this Vertue, in honour of the blessed Virgin, saying,

O Soveraign Queen ! I contemplate you as the hope of the World ; long expected by the Fathers in Limbo ; earnestly look'd upon by the Souls suffering in Purgatory ; humbly besought by the Children of the Church Militant.

In this number I rank my self and place in you (O holy Virgin !) next after God, my hope and confidence, trusting that you will be to me a Fountain of Grace, a Tower of Defence, a City of Refuge, a Gate of Heaven to give me entrance unto Paradise.

Receive (most sacred Lady !) this Emerald, which I present unto you for your Crown, and strengthen my hope unto the end; Ave Maria, Gratia Plena, &c.

3. *The Ruby of Charity :* Produce

Acts proper to this Vertue, saying,

O *Soveraign Queen! I consider you as brim full of perfect Love and Charity, and inviting the whole world to participate with you of its sweet fruits and effects:* saying, *come to me, all you who desire me, and be replenished with my generations,* Eccle.24.

Behold, *I come to you with an ardent and enflam'd affection, beseeching you to enrich me with the treasure of true Charity towards God and my Neighbour.*

Receive (*most sacred Lady!*) *this* Ruby, *which I offer unto you for your Crown, and confirm my love and charity to the end.* Amen. Ave Maria, &c.

4. The *Diamond of Fortitude :* Produce the Acts belonging to this vertue, saying,

O *Soveraign Queen! I behold you as a valiant Champion: terrible (to the Troops of Satan) like a well order'd Army. Encourage me, I beseech you, to fight under your banner ; support my weakness with your strong hand, and help me to overcome all worldly, fleshly, and diabolical temptations, &c.*

Receive [*most sacred Lady !*] *this* Diamond, *which I present unto you for your Crown, and obtain for me an invincible Fortitude to the end,* Amen. Ave Ma-

3. *The Pearl of Chastity:* Produce Acts appertaining to this vertue, saying,

O Soveraign Queen! I admire you as the Mother of Purity, the Mirrour of Chastity, the first who vow'd Virginity: obtain for me I beseech you, that all my thoughts, words and actions, may savour of Purity, be season'd with modesty, and be accompany'd with Chastity, &c.

Receive [*most sacred Lady!*] *this Pearl, which I present unto you to illustrate your Crown, and powerfully protect me against all carnality, and impurity to the end.* Amen. Ave Maria, &c.

4. *The fourth Exercise,* may be to practice some particular devotion upon such days as are dedicated to the blessed Virgins memory and honour, which are all the *Saturdays* besides the rest of her annual Festivities; These devotions may be to visit her Altar, to recite her Litanies, to make use of some of these [or the like] prescribed forms, &c.

5. *The fifth Exercise,* may be the paying of some Annual Tribute [as St. *Peter Damian* tearms it] to the blessed Virgin, [how little soever it be] in token of the homage and servitude due to her,

Soveraign Empire: This tribute may be tendered at some Altar, dedicated to her honour, together with the recital of this Prayer.

Receive [O *Soveraign Empress!*] this small Tribute, which I here most humbly present to your sacred Majesty, in acknowledgement of that supreme Dominion, you have [next after God] over my heart; and to testifie the desire I have to live and die your Bond slave; Permit not [O sacred Virgin!] that I ever pay unto Sathan, the World, or my sensuality, any Tribute of Sin: and procure for me a happy passage from this my earthly Pilgrimage, to the Heavenly Paradise: there to offer up to your Son and You, an Eternal Tribute of praise and benediction. *Amen.*

6. *The sixth Exercise,* may be that of Penance and Mortification, by directly taking a Discipline, or wearing some harsh thing upon the bare skin &c. at certain times of the year, according to each ones strength of body, and the counsel of his ghostly Father, reciting upon such days seven times the *Salve Regina,* in memory of the blessed Virgins seven sorrows: and adding this Prayer taken out of St. *Peter Damian.*

O my most glorious Lady: the Mirrour

N 2

rour of purity, and pattern of all vertue !
I wretched Sinner, do most humbly acknowledge that I have highly offended
your Son and You, by the foolish and
besotted liberty of my body and soul ;
and therefore having now no other refuge left me, I here prostrate my heart
before you ; [O my compassionate Mother !] bequeathing my self unto you in
quality of a Bond-slave, and submitting
my whole self to your holy Empire, and
command. Curb, I beseech you, this rebellious body of mine, receive this con-
tumacious and stubborn heart, and let
not your mercie reject me a sinner, since
your Immaculate Virginity brought
forth the Author of all Piety.

A concluding Prayer to the sacred Virgin-
Mother upon the same subject.

O Holy Virgin, Mother of God !
Queen of Men and Angels! Marvel
of Heaven and Earth ! I reverence you
in all the ways that I can according to
God, that I should according to your
own Greatness, and according as your
divine Son Christ *Jesus* our Lord would
have you reverenc'd upon Earth and in
Heaven.

I make to you an Oblation of my

foul and my life, and will belong to you
for evermore ; and I will render you
some *particular* Homage and Dependency in all future time and Eternity.

O Mother of grace and mercy ! I make
choice of you for the Mother of my foul,
in honour of that choice which God
himfelf made of you for the *Mother* of
his Son.

O Queen of Men and Angels. . I ac-
cept and acknowledge you for my Soveraign Mother, in honour of that Dependency, which my Saviour and my God
had on you as upon his Mother; And in
this Quality, I bequeath unto you all
power over my foul, and over my life, as
much as (according to God) I can bequeath it.

O facred Virgin Mother ! look upon
me as upon your *own thing,* and in your
goodnefs ufe me as the *Subject* of your
power, and as the *Object* of your pity.

O Source of *Life!* Fountain of *Grace!*
Refuge of *Sinners!* I have recourfe unto
you, hoping thereby to be freed from *fin,*
furnifhed with *Grace,* and preferved
from eternal *Death.*

that which I deſerve not to obtain, by reaſon of my offences : and let the *laſt hour* of my Life (*that hour* which is to decide my Eternity) be in your hands, in honour of that happy *Moment* of the *Incarnation*, wherein God became Man, and you were made Gods Mother.

O Virgin, and O Mother both together ! O ſacred Temple of the ſoveraign Deity ! O Mervail of Heaven and of Earth ! O glorious Mother of my God! I am yours by the general *Title* of your greatneſs ; but I will be alſo yours by the particular *Title* of my own choice, and by this act of my own free will. Wherefore I give my ſelf to you, and to your Son Chriſt Jeſus my Lord and Saviour, and I reſolve to let paſs no day without rendring to him and to you ſome particular homage, and ſome ſpecial reſtification of this my dependency and ſervitude, in which my deſire is to die and to live for evermore.

The Litanies of our Blessed Lady of Loretto.

So called,

For that they are usually sung in that sacred Church of Loretto, *upon all the Saturdays in the year, (as they are also in this our Chappel of the Rosary) and Feasts of the Blessed Virgin* Mary.

THE pious Rosarists may please to take notice, that some years since there were *certain Religious Persons,* who agreed together to recite daily these holy Litanies for the happy death of each other; to whom many thousands joyn'd themselves, throughout all *Italy, Spain, France, Germany,* and the *Indies.* And why should not the like sacred Association be established also in our Countrey, amongst such devout Christians as are equally zealous of the Blessed Virgins honour, and as much desirous of a happy death?

We therefore (the Compilers of this Book) do hereby declare unto all you, (the devout Children and Servants of our Common-Mother the ever Blessed Virgin *Mary*) that we intend henceforth

to recite daily these following Litanies
for each others happy death: And that
we do now, (even by these presents,
without any further declaration or ceremony) admit, receive, and associate
unto our selves, and to a joint commu-
nication with us in these our Prayers;
All such as being desirous thereof, shall
mutually perform these *three* following points.

1. Recite daily these Litanies, with
the adjoyned Anthem and Prayer, to
the sacred Virgin, and to Saint *Joseph.*

2. Recite them for all such as are
thus associated, as they all recite the same
for him.

3. Recite them for his own and their
happy death, and for the obtaining of
grace necessary for that purpose.

Litaniæ Beatæ Mariæ Virginis Lau-
retana.

Antiphona.

Sub tuum præsidium confugimus (San-
cta Dei Genitrix!) nostras deprecati-
ones ne despicias in necessitatibus nostris,
sed a periculis cunctis, libera nos semper

Virgo gloriosa & benedicta; Domina no-
stra, Mediatrix nostra, Advocata nostra ;
tuo Filio nos reconcilia, tuo filio nos re-
commenda, tuo Filio nos representa, nunc
& in hora mortis nostra.

> *Kyrie eleison.*
> *Christe eleison.*
> *Kyrie eleison.*
> *Christe audi nos.*
> *Christe exaudi nos.*

Pater de Cœlis Deus,
Fili Redemptor mundi Deus,
Spiritus Sancte Deus,
Sancta Trinitas unus Deus,
Sancta Maria,
Sancta Dei Genitrix,
Sancta Virgo Virginum,
Mater Christi,
Mater divinæ gratiæ,
Mater purissima,
Mater castissima,
Mater inviolata,
Mater intemerata,
Mater amabilis,
Mater admirabilis,
Mater Creatoris,
Mater Salvatoris,
Virgo Prudentissima,
Virgo Veneranda,
Virgo Predicanda,
Virgo potens,

miserere nobis

Ora pro nobis

Virgo Clemens,
Virgo Fidelis,
Speculum justitiæ,
Sedes Sapientiæ,
Causa nostræ lætitiæ,
Vas spirituale,
Vas honorabile,
Vas insigne Devotionis,
Rosa mystica,
Turris Davidica,
Turris Eburnea,
Domus Aurea,
Fœderis Arca,
Ianua Cœli,
Stella Matutina,
Salus infirmorum,
Refugium Peccatorum,
Consolatrix Afflictorum,
Auxilium Christianorum,
Regina Angelorum,
Regina Patriarcharum,
Regina Prophetarum,
Regina Apostolorum,
Regina Martyrum,
Regina Confessorum,
Regina Virginum,
Regina Sanctorum omnium,
Regina sacratissimi Rosarii,

Ora pro nobis.

Agnus Dei, qui tollis peccata mundi,
Parce nobis Domine.
Agnus Dei, qui tollis peccata mundi,

Exaudi nos Domine.
Agnus Dei qui tollis peccata mundi,.
Miserere nobis.

Antiphona.

*S*Ub tuum præsidium confugimus sancta Dei genitrix, nostras deprecationes ne despicias in necessitatibus nostris, sed a periculis cunctis libera nos semper Virgo gloriosa & benedicta; Domina nostra, Mediatrix nostra, Advocata nostra! tuo Filio nos reconcilia, tuo Filio nos recommenda, tuo Filio nos repræsenta, nunc, & in hora mortis nostræ.

Ver. *Ora pro nobis sancta Dei Genitrix.*

Resp. *Ut digni efficiamur promissionibus Christi.*

Oremus.

*M*Emorare, O piissima Virge Maria! non esse auditum a seculo, quenquam ad tua confugientem præsidia, tua implorantem auxilia, tua petentem suffragia a te esse derelictum.

Versus & Oratio de Sancto Josepho.

Vers. *Justus ut palma florebit.*
Resp. *Sicut Cedrus Libani multiplica-*
bitur.

Oremus.

Sanctissima Genitricis tuæ Sponsi, quæsumus Domine, meritis adjuvemur; ut
quod possibilitas nostra non obtinet, ejus nobis intercessione donetur. Qui vivis &
regnas in sæcula sæculorum.
Ans. *Amen.*

The Litanies of our Blessed Lady of Loretto.

Anthem.

VVE flie to your Patronage (O
sacred Mother of God l) de-
spise not our Prayers in our necessities,
but deliver us from all dangers, O ever
glorious and Blessed Virgin l Our Lady,
our Mediatrix, our Advocate l Reconcile us to your Son, recommend us to
your Son, represent us to your Son,
now, and at the hour of our death.
Lord have mercy upon us.
Christ have mercy upon us.

Lord have mercy upon us.

Christ hear us.

   O Christ graciously hear us.

God the Father of Heaven,

   Have mercy upon us.

God the Son, Redeemer of the world,

   Have mercy upon us.

God the holy Ghost,

   Have mercy upon us.

O holy Trinity, one God,

   Have mercy upon us.

Holy *Mary*,
Holy Mother of God,
Holy Virgin of Virgins,
Mother of Christ,
Mother of divine Grace,
Mother most pure,
Mother most chast,
Mother undefiled,
Mother untouched,
Mother most amiable,
Mother most admirable,
Mother of our Creator,
Mother of our Redeemer,
Virgin most Prudent,
Virgin most Venerable,
Virgin most renowned,
Virgin most Powerful,
Virgin most Merciful,
Virgin most Faithful,

Pray for us.

Mirrour of Justice,
Seat of Wisdom,
Cause of our Joy,
Spiritual Vessel,
Honourable Vessel,
Vessel of singular Devotion,
Mystical Rose,
Tower of *David*,
Tower of Ivory,
House of Gold,
Ark of the Covenant,
Gate of Heaven,
Morning Star,
Health of the Weak,
Refuge of Sinners,
Comfort of the Afflicted,
Help of Christians,
Queen of Angels,
Queen of Patriarchs,
Queen of Prophets,
Queen of Apostles,
Queen of Martyrs,
Queen of Confessors,
Queen of Virgins,
Queen of all Saints,
Queen of the most sacred Rosary,

Pray for us.

   Lamb of God, who takest away the
   sins of the world,
     Spare us, O Lord,
   Lamb of God, who takest away the
   sins of the world,

Lamb of God, who takest away the
sins of the World,
Have mercy on us.

Anthem.

WE fly to your *Patronage* (O *sacred
Mother of God!*) *Despise not our
prayers in our necessities, but deliver us
from all dangers, O ever glorious and Blessed Virgin, our Lady, our Mediatrix, our
Advocate! Reconcile us to your Son, Recommend us to your Son, Represent us to
your Son, now, and at the hour of our death.*
Ver. Pray for us, O holy Mother of God.
   *Ans. That we may become worthy of
Christs promises.*

Let us pray.

REmember (O most compassionate
Virgin *Mary!* Mother of Power,
Mercy, and Consolation!) That it was
never yet heard or known, that any one
was by you rejected, who in his grievous
pressures, and afflictions, had recourse to
your powerful Prayers, Patronage, and
Protection :
   Imboldened with this confidence, we
your distressed Children of the holy
Rosary, with eyes full of tears, and

hearts full of forrow, make now to you (O facred Virgin Mother!) our moft humble addreffes in thefe our prefent and preffing neceffities.

Defpife not our words, we befeech you (O Bleffed Mother of the Word Eternal and Incarnate!) reject not thé Petitions of your poor fervants,(O you pious Comforter of all afflicted fonls!) but gracioufly vouchfafe to hear us, to help us,to protect us, and to obtain for us the accomplifhment of all our juft and humble defires; That we may have frefh occafion to admire your tranfcendent Mercy, Charity, and Compaffion, and to magnifie and praife with eternal gratitude and thankfgiving, the infinite goodnefs of your Divine *Son*, our fweet Saviour, Chrift Jefus.

The *Verfe* and *Prayer* of St. Jofeph.

Verf. The juft man fhall flourifh as a Palm-tree.

An. *He fhall be multiplied as the Cedar of Libanus.*

Let us pray.

A Ssift us, O Lord, we befeech thee, by the merits of Saint *Jofeph*, thy facred Mothers Bridegroom; that

what we are unworthy to obtain, may
be granted us by his intercession: who
livest and reignest world without end.

Missa votiva per anni Circulum Sanctissimi Rosarii Beatæ Virginis, quam
hic imprimi fecimus, propterea quod
in perpaucis Missalibus reperiatur.

*S*Alve Sancta Parens enixa puerpera
Regem: Qui Cœlum terramque regit
in sacula seculorum.

Ver. Post partum virgo inviolata permansisti: Dei Genitrix intercede pro nobis.
Gloria Patri, &c.

Oratio.

*D*Eus cujus unigenitus per vitam mortem, & Resurrectionem in nostra
carnis substantia, nobis salutis eterna præmia comparavit: Da famulis tuis hac
omnia per sancto Rosarium recensentibus, imitari q̃ odgessit, sentire qua pertulit, & assequi quod promisit. Per eundem, &c.

Lectio Libri Sapientiæ.

*A*B initio, & ante secula creata sum, &
usque ad futurum seculum non desi-
nam, & in habitatione sancta coram ipso
ministravi; & sic in Sion firmata sum,
& in civitate sanctificata similiter re-
quievi, & in Jerusalem potestas mea. Et

raditæ in populo honorificato, & in parte Dei mei hereditas illius, & in plenitudine Sanctorum detentio mea.

Resp. Benedicta & venerabilis es virgo Maria: quæ sine tactu pudoris inventa es mater Salvatoris.

Vers. Virgo Dei genitrix, quem totus non capit orbis, in tua se clausit viscera factus homo. Alleluja.

Alleluja. Virga Jesse floruit, virgo Deum & hominem genuit: pacem Deus reddidit, in se reconcilians ima summis. Alleluja.

Infra Septuagesimam.

Gaude Maria virgo, cunctas hæreses sola interemisti.

Tempore Paschali.

Alleluja. Virga Jesse floruit. ut supra.

Alleluja. Surrexit Dominus & occurrens mulieribus ait, avete: tunc accesserunt, & tenuerunt pedes ejus.

Tempore Ascensionis. Alleluja.

Ascendens Christus in altum captivam duxit captivitatem: Dedit dona hominibus.

Sequentia sancti Evangelii secundum Lucam, Luk, 11.

In illo tempore Loquente Jesu ad turbas, extollens vocem quædam mulier de turba, dixit illi: Beatus venter,

qui te portavit ; & ubera quæ suxisti, at
ille dixit : Quin immo beati, qui audiunt
verbum Dei, & custodiunt illud.

Offertorium.

Ave Regina cœlorum: Mater Regis
Angelorum. O Maria flos virginum, ve-
lut rosa vel Lilium, funde preces ad filium,
pro salute fidelium.

Secreta.

Fac nos quæ sumus Domine, his muneri-
bus offerendis convenienter aptari, &
per sancti Rosarii mysteria sacratissima
fidei mysteriorum coronantes, sic recensere
præterita & præsentia dolere, atque cura fu-
turorum pignora capiamus.

Communio.

Beata viscera Mariæ virginis, quæ
portaverunt æterni patris filium. Alleluia.

Post communio.

Veneranda Sacratissimi Rosarii
Mysteria in honorem Dei genetricis semperque virginis Mariæ, ab Ecclesia tua
fideli dicata celebrantes omnipotens Deus,
benigno favore prosequere: & omnibus in
te sperantibus, auxilii tui munus ostende:
& Mysteriorum virtus, & votorum obti-
neatur effectus. Per eundem Dominum
nostrum Iesum Christum filium suum, Qui
tecum, &c. Ite Missa est. Vel Benedica-
mus Domino.

Several Prayers.

Whereof one or more may be sometimes added after the Litanies of our Blessed Lady, according to each ones Devotion, Occasion, or Necessity.

1.
A Prayer for our Soveraign King
CHARLES.

O Almighty God, King of Kings, and Lord of Lords, from whom all power in heaven and earth is derived! We most humbly beseech you to look in mercy upon our most gracious Soveraign King *Charles*, whom your divine goodness hath wonderfully restored to his people, and re-established in the Royal Seat of his worthy Predecessors, to govern under you these Kingdoms: Give him prudence O Lord! to know your holy will, and grace to practice it; Preserve him from all danger, defend him from all his enemies, bless him here with peace, plenty, and prosperity upon Earth, and bring him hereafter to your eternal joy and felicity in Heaven, through Jesus Christ our Lord. *Amen.*

2.

A Prayer for our Gracious Queen CATHERINE.

ALmighty and all-merciful Creator, we most humbly offer up our Prayers to your divine Majesty in behalf of your Servant, our Gracious Queen *Catherine*, whom your Providence hath associated to the Royal Throne of these Kingdoms.

Give her, we beseech you, true zeal to promote your honour, sincere Piety to perform her duty, solid Prudence in her comportment towards all persons, faithful Constancy in all troubles and temptations, a happy Issue for the comfort and peace of her People, and all such gifts, graces, and vertues, as are proper for the discharge of her High Place and Dignitie ; that after she hath here reigned prosperously amongst us upon Earth, she may hereafter reign perpetually amongst your glorious Saints in Heaven: Through the merits of your dear Son, our Lord and Saviour Christ Jesus. *Amen.*

3.

*A Filial Recommendation of our selves
to the sacred Virgin-Mothers
protection.*

O Sacred and Soveraign Lady-Mother, (next after God) the only hope
of my Soul) Into that singular faith,
commendation, and custody, whereby
your tenderlie loving Son, Christ Jesus
my Saviour, recommended you from the
Cross to his dearly beloved Disciple
St. *John*: I do this day, and all the daies
of my life, commend and commit my
body, my soul, my senses, my honour,
all my hope and comfort, all my angui-
shes, miseries, and afflictions, all my
thoughts, words, and actions, my whole
life, and the final end thereof: Most
humbly beseeching you, that I may (by
your powerful intercession) be preserved from all sin, from all scandal, from
whatsoever may any way displease
yours, or your Sons pure eyes, provoke
your anger, or hazard the loss of your
favour, and from a sudden and unprovided death. Obtain for me, I beseech
you, (O my glorious Lady-Mother l)
that I may be truly penitent for all my
past offences, that I may manfully resist
all present occasions of sin, that I may

walk more warilie and innocentlie for the future.

Let me feel your prompt and powerfull assistance during the whole course of this my lives Pilgrimage; and in the dreadful day of my judgment, be you pleased (O sacred Mother!) to become my pious Advocatrix at the Tribunal of your Son Christ Jesus: To whom, with the Father and the Holy Ghost, be all honour and glory for evermore, *Amen.*

4.
A Prayer for a happy death.

O My dear Lord Jesu! I most humblie beseech you by those most bitter pains and pangs which you suffered for me in your cruel Passion, and particularlie in the hour wherein your Divine Soul passed forth of your blessed Body; take pitie upon my poor and sinful soul in its last agonie, and in its passage to Eternitie.

And you, O compassionate Virgin-Mother *Mary!* remember how you sadly stood by your deer Son dying on the Cross, and by that your excessive grief, and your Sons sacred death, assist my soul in its last conflict with death, and conduct it to a happie Eternitie.

And you, O glorious Saints, *John,*

Joseph, Nicodemus, Lazarus, Mary Magdalen, Mary of James, Mary of Salome, and Martha, who stood by my dear Redeemer Christ Jesus expiring on the Cross; assist me also in the hour of my souls departure, and accompanie it to a happie Eternitie. Amen.

5.

A general Prayer, for our Selves, our Friends, and the whole Church.

DIssolve we beseech you, O Lord, by your bountie, the bonds of our sins; and by the intercession of the sacred Virgin, and all your blessed Saints, preserve us, our Friends, our Brethren, and our Benefactors, in your grace and sanctitie: Purge, O Lord, from all impietie, and enrich with solid vertues and perfections, all such as have any relation to us by consanguinitie, affinitie, or familiaritie; grant us health of body peace of mind, quiet of conscience; assist us against all our visible and invisible adversaries; destroy in us all carnal and worldly desires; impart wholsomnes unto the air, and to the Earth fruitfulnes; unite the hearts both of our Friends, and of our Enemies, in true love and charitie; defend our Gracious Queen *Catherine*, and all them of ourConfraternitie of the sacred Rosary, from all contagious diseases, from all plaguy infection, and from all heretical crueltie and incursion. Protect our chief Pastor, our Superiours, the Clergie, and the whole Body of the Catholique Church, from all miserie and adversitie; give prosperitie to the living, and rest to the departed; and let your divine blessing be upon us all this day, and evermore. *Amen.*

6.

A Prayer for the conversion of Hereticks and Infidels.

O Almightie and all-merciful God! who seekest and desirest the salvation of all souls; Take pitie (we beseech you) upon all such as are seduced with pestiferous errours, and segregated from the unity of your sacred Church; Pardon them, O Lord! for they perceive not what they do; Illuminate the eyes of their understanding, O true light of all spirits! that they may see their own blindness, and seeing it, may speedilie abandon it; and that so becoming sincerelie reconciled to you the supream Shepherd, and to your Church the only safe Sheep-fold, they may joyfullie praise and magnifie your mercies, together with us your faithful Children, for evermore. *Amen.*

7.

A Prayer for a special Friend.

PReserve, O Lord! this your servant, and our Benefactor *N.* for whom we humblie offer up these our Petitions to your sacred Majestie; beseeching you to grant him a perseverant constancie in the Catholick Faith, a safe passage through this lives dangerous pilgrimage, and that no worldlie, carnal, or diabolical temptations may have the power to separate him from you his prime and only good.

Pardon his sins we beseech you, whereby he hath deserved your indignation; Increase his justice, due to your self, and to his neighbour; give him grace to correspond to the calling and condition wherein you have placed him; let him be equallie moderate, patient, resigned in adversitie, and in prosperitie; direct him in all his waies, and defend him against all his enemies, and grant him finallie a happie death and departure out of this world, and a speedie passage after death to the fruition of your eternal felicitie.

8.

A Prayer for a Friend in Tribulation.

VOuchsafe (we beseech you, O merciful Creator !) to afford the sweetness of your consolation to your afflicted servant *N.* Remove (O Lord) according to your good pleasure, the heavie burthen of his calamities ; give him patience in his sufferings, resignation to your providence, perseverance in your service, and a happy translation from this calamitous life to eternal glorie.

9.

A Prayer for a Friend in his sickness and infirmitie.

O Soveraign Lord God ! the Author of our health, and our comfort in sickness ; in the watch of whose divine providence run all the moments of our lives earthlie pilgrimage ! Hear (we beseech you) the prayers which we pour out before you for *N.* your infirm, but faithful servant ; and mercifullie restore him to his former welfare, that he may henceforth walk more worthy of his calling, and make greater progress in Christian vertue and pietie. But if it be your pleasure (O supream Lord of life

nitie, let your moſt juſt will (O heavenlie Father!) be accompliſhed in this,
and in all things whatſoever; only let
Death find him well prepared, and
rightly diſpoſed! Let him humblie kiſs
your paternal rod which chaſtiſeth him,
and patientlie ſubmit to the croſs which
your loving hand hath laid upon his
ſhoulders; let him behave himſelf, during the remaining time of his infirmity,
as befits a pious and devout Chriſtian;
free from puſillanimitie and deſpair, full
of hope and filial confidence: And finallie, being ſtrengthned with the Sacraments, reconciled to his Fnemies,
and ſetled in your grace and favour, let
him chearfullie expect, and joyfullie embrace Deaths ſummons, and his bodies
and ſouls ſeparation. *Amen.*

10.

*A Prayer for our Enemies, Detractors,
and Perſecutors.*

OMeek and merciful Lord Jeſu! the
great Maſter, Exemplar, and Practi-
ſer of Peace, Charitie, and Union
amongſt men! Who haſt commanded us
to love our Enemies, and to do good for
them that hate us, and who prayed on
the Croſr for your capital Adverſaries;
increaſe within us (we moſt humblie

beseech you) the spirit of Christian charitie, meeknes, and sweetnes; that we may freelie, sincerelie, and heartilie forgive all such as have any way offended us, injured us, or persecuted us; and that we may conquer all our Enemies malice by our fraternal compassion and affection: Bestow on them also, (O blessed Saviour!) the same spirit of perfect peace, love, and charitie; and powerfullie defend us from all their treacherie and deceits. *Amen.*

II.

A Prayer for a Woman great with Child, or labouring in Child-bed.

O Most dread Soveraign! who for the just punishment of the first Womans prevarication, have pronounced and imposed a severe and unavoydable sentence of malediction, upon all Woman-kind to wit, that they should conceive their Children in Original sin; that having conceived them, they should be subject to many miseries; and that they should bring them forth with the hazard of their own lives: we most humblie beseech you, (O undrainable Fountain of goodnes and mercie!) that you will be graciouslie pleased by your Blessed Mothers pious intercession, to

mitigate the rigorous Edict of this general Law in behalf of this your poor
Handmaid, (now labouring in the pangs
of Child-bed) and to give her courage,
comfort, and patience in her sorrows.
Grant that in due time she may be hap-
pilie and speedilie delivered; that the
Child she bears in her Womb, may be
brought forth into the world, accompanied with all such perfections of body,
soul, and senses, as are befitting our humane nature, that it may live to be re-
born by sacred Baptism, and that both
the Child and the Mother may become
your faithful servants. *Amen.*

12.

*A Prayer to appease the Divine Indigna-
tion, in any publick or private necessity.*

WHen we compare, O Lord! your
punishments with our own im-
pieties, we are forced to confess, that our
crimes do far exceed your chastisements.
We are sensible of our sins penaltie, but
we leave not our sinful pertinacie; our
sick minds are troubled, but our stiff
necks are not bowed; our life langui-
shes under the burden of our afflictions,
and yet we amend not our wicked actions; we acknowledge our misdeeds in
the day of correction, and we forget

what we bewailed after the visitation.
If you, O Lord! stretch forth your hand
to strike us, we make you large promises; if you sheath your sword, we fail in
our performances. If you scourge us, we
petition you to spare us; if you mercifullie spare us, we again malicioussie provoke you to scourge us.

Behold, O dread Soveraign! you have
us self-accused, adjudged, condemned;
and we well know, that unless you will
pardon us, we must needs perish.

Grant unto us (O compassionate Father!) that which we desire, though we
deserve it not, who hast given us a being when we were not. *Amen.*

13.

*A Prayer to withdraw our minds from
the superfluous cares and solicitudes of this World.*

O Lord, our true Lover, our faithful
Teacher, our bountiful Nourisher!
Take from us all vain, superfluous, and
noxious cares and solicitudes; and since
you have been graciously pleased to promise us, that your self will make a sufficient provision for us, grant that we may
confidentlie relie in all things upon your
sacred providence. Let us therefore fix
our hearts and affections upon heaven-

lie objects; let us seek only your Kingdom, and be only solicitous for the advancement of your honour and glorie; let us run on chearfullie, couragiouslie, perseverantlie, in the way of your precepts, during our earthlie pilgrimage, that so we may be finallie tranflated to your heavenlie Paradife. *Amen.*

14.

Prayers to be said in time of the Plague.

The Anthem.

REmember your Covenant (O merciful Creator!) and say to the smiting Angel, *Now hold thy hand;* that the Earth may not become desolate, and every living foul destroyed.

Verf. Lord let your anger cease from your People.

An. And from your City.

Let us pray.

HEar (we beseech you, O compassionate Lord God!) the Prayers of your People; and as we confess our selves to be justly afflicted for our offences, so be you pleased in mercy to free us, for the glory of your own sacred name.

O God! who well knows that our
humane

humane frailtie cannot subsist amidst so
many and great dangers, without the
support of your divine favour and assistance. Give us (we beseech you) health
of mind and body; and grant that we
may overcome by your help and mercie,
what we deservedlie suffer for our own
sins and impieties.

Lord! lend a gracious ear to the petitions of your poor servants, grant them
the desired effect of their faithful supplications, and avert from us the furie of
the raging Pestilence; whereby the
hearts of all mortal men may humblie
and gratefullie acknowledge, that such
scourges proceed from your just anger
and indignation, and cease through your
boundless mercie and goodness.

A Prayer to the sacred Virgin-Mother, called the Miraculous Prayer against the Plague.

THe Star of Heaven, (whose snowy
    breast,
Did suckle our (sweet Lord!) supprest
The Plague of Death, whose origen
Was from the very first of men:
May that clear Star at present daign
Those Constellations to restrain;

Whose wars deprive men of their
 breath,
By the destructive wound of Death.

Repeat thrice these ensuing Verses.

Bright Star o'th' Sea, 'gainst Plague your
 help afford,
Nought is deny'd you by your Son, our
 Lord,
Who honours you, Blest Maid: us, Jesu,
 save,
Which for us, at your hands, she daigns
 to crave.

Let us pray.

O God of mercie, God of compassion, God of Pardon! who in time
past taking pity upon your afflicted people, gave command to the striking Angel, that he should with-hold his hand
from further punishing them: we most
humblie beseech you, for the love of that
glorious Star, whose sacred Breasts you
most sweetly suck'd, that you will
vouchsafe us your gracious help, whereby we may be preserved from all Plaguy
infection delivered from an unprovided
death, and secured from all destructive
accidents and incursions. Amen.

15.

*A most devout and efficacious Prayer to
the sacred Virgin-Mother; in the honour of her blessed Sons Passion, and her
own Compassion: to be recited with a
pure devotion and perfect Resignation,
for the space of 30. daies; in hopes to
obtain of the divine Mercy, a full grant
of all lawful demands.*

HOly Mary! Perpetual Virgin,
Mother of Power, Grace, and Mercy! Sweet Comfort of all sad, desolate,
and distressed persons!

By that Sword of sorrow which
pierced your soul, when your dear Son
our Saviour Christ Jesus, suffered a cruel
Death upon the Cross, and by that Filial affection wherewith he reciprocally
compassionating your maternal affliction, recommended you to the care of his
beloved Disciple St. John; take pity and
compassion upon me (I beseech you) in
this my present and pressing affliction, infirmitie, povertie, and whatsoever other
spiritual or corporal necessitie.

O assured Refuge of all miserable
wretches! Hear my prayers, behold
my tears, consider my sorrows, and so
mediate my misericie; for God I find my

self encompassed with these grievous afflictions and calamities by reason of my
great crimes and offences ; I know not
whither to fly for succour, or to whom
I may make my moan, but to you my
meek and merciful Mother.

Lend therefore (I beseech you, *O loving Mother!*) the Ears of your ordina-
rie pietie, and wonted mercie ; to the
humble Petition of your poor child and
servant.

And by the powels of your dear Son
Jesus: By that sweetness which his blessed soul resented at the time of his alli-
ance with our humane nature ; when
resolving with the Father and the Holy
Ghost, to unite his divine person to
mortal flesh for mans salvation, he sent
his Angel to you (*O holy Virgin!*) with
these happie tidings ; and the Holy
Ghost over-shadowing you, clad himself
with our humanitie in your chast en-
trals ; remaining true God and true
man for the space of nine Months in
your sacred Womb ; and from thence
vouchsafed to visit the world :

By the anguish, which this your same
dear Son, our Blessed Saviour Christ
Jesus, endured ; when (the time of
his designed Passion drawing nigh,)
he prayed to his eternal Father upon

Mount *Olivet*, That if it might stand with his divine providence, this bitter Chalice might pass away from him:

By this thrice-repeated Prayer of his, and all the painful Journeys he undertook in the time of his Passion, in which you, (his compassionate Mother!) dolefullie followed him from place to place, never leaving him till his last gasp upon Mount *Calvary*:

By the outragious injuries, scornful disgraces, cruel blows, contumelious blasphemies, forged witnesses, false accusations, and unjust judgments, which he (innocent Lamb!) patientlie endured.

By the shackles which fettered his Limbs, the tears which flowed from his Eyes, the bloud which trickled from his whole Bodie:

By the Fear, the Sorrow, and the Sadness of his heart, and by the shame he received, in being stripp'd of his garments, to hang naked upon the Cross in your presence, (*O sorrowful Virgin!*) and in the sight of all the people:

By his Royal head, crowned with Thorns, and smitten with a Reed; By his Thirst, quenched with Vinegar and gall: By his side opened with a spear, and issuing forth bloud and water, to refresh our souls with the living Fountain of his

By the sharp Nailes, wherewith his tender Hands and Feet were cruellie pierced, and fastned to the Cross.

By the recommendation of his departing Soul to his Eternal Father; saying, Into your hands, (*O my heavenly Father!*) I commend my Spirit.

By his giving up the Ghost, when he cryed out with a loud voice; *My God, my God, why have you forsaken me* : And then bowing down his blessed head, said: *All is finished* :

By the great Mercie he shewed towards the good Thiet; by his Descent into *Limbus*, and the Joy he communicated to the just Souls there detained:

By the glory of his triumphant Resurrection, and the comfortable appiritions he frequently made for Forty days space to you (*O sacred Virgin!*) to his holy Apostles, and to his other chosen friends and servants:

By his admirable Ascension, when in yours and his Apostles sight, he was elevated into heaven:

By the miraculous coming down of the Holy Ghost in form of fierie tongues; wherewith he replenished the hearts of his Disciples; and encouraged them to plant his Faith in the whole world:

By the dreadful day of general judgment, in which he is to give sentence upon all mankind.

By the mutual compassions, and tender affections you had towards each other, whilst you liv'd together in this world.

By the unspeakable joy of your glorious Assumption; when in the presence, and by the power of your blessed Son, you were taken up into Heaven, to be with him made partaker of his eternal felicity.

By all these Sorrows, Joys, Passions, Compassions, and whatsoever is near and dear to you in Heaven, and upon Earth; take pity upon me (*O compassionate Mother!*) hear my Prayer, and help me to obtain of your all-powerful, and all-merciful Son, that for which I now most humbly and heartily petition him.

Mention here the thing which you desire; or reflect mentally upon it.

ANd as I am most certainly assured, that your dear Son, who so highly honours you, will not refuse to hear your prayers, and grant your request; so let me (I beseech you, O *blessed Mother!*) fully, speedily and efficaciously, feel the help and succour of your compassionate heart, and your merciful Sons most perfect will and pleasure; who grants the petitions of them that fear and love him, even to their own souls desire and satisfaction.

Behold me therefore (*O pious Mother!*) in these my present necessities, and especially in this, for which I have now humbly invok'd your sacred Name, and heartily implor'd your powerful assistance.

Obtain also for me (*O my dear Mother!*) of your divine Son, a constant Faith, a confident Hope, a perfect Charity, a cordial Contrition a sincere Confession, a sufficient satisfaction, a diligent Custody of my self from future fallings, an heroique Contempt of the world, a compleat Conquest of my Passions, and over my Ghostly enemies, a zealous Imitation of yours and your Sons exemplarie life and conversation, a willing readiness to die for yours and his love and honour, an entire accomplishment of my Vows, an absolute Mortification of my self-will, a filial Perseverance in Grace and good works, a happy departure of my soul out of this world, with my perfect senses about me, the holy Sacraments to comfort me, and your self

(*O sacred Mother!*) with the Saints my particular Patrons, and my good Angel to conduct me to eternal rest, eternal life, eternal happiness. *Amen.*

16.

The Prayer of Pope Sixtus *the fourth to the Blessed Virgin; who also granted great Indulgences to such as shall devoutly recite it, before her holy Picture.*

ALl Hail, O most holy *Mary!* the Mother of God, the Queen of heaven, the Gate of Paradise, the Lady of the world. You are that singularly pure Creature, who, being your self conceiv'd without sin, conceiv'd Christ Jesus without blemish. Pray for us to your all-powerful Son; protect us from all evil, defend our Gracious Queen *Catherine,* and all the devout Rosarists of this holy confraternity, from all contagious diseases, from all plaguy infection, and from all heretical cruelty and incursion. *Amen.*

17.

A Prayer to the Blessed Virgin, of great vertue and efficacy against a sudden, impenitent, and unprovided death.

HAil *Mary!* the handmaid of the Holy Trinity.

Hail

Hail *Mary!* the eternally chosen Daughter of God the Father.

Hail *Mary!* the Mother of our Lord Jesus Christ,

Hail *Mary!* the Spouse of the Holy Ghost.

Hail *Mary!* the Sister of the Angels.

Hail *Mary!* the Promise of the Prophets.

Hail *Mary!* the Queen of the Patriarks.

Hail *Mary!* the Mistris of the Evangelists.

Hail *Mary!* the Teacher of the Apostles.

Hail *Mary!* the Comforter of the Martyrs.

Hail *Mary!* the Fountain and fulness of the Confessors.

Hail *Mary!* the Crown and Ornament of the Virgins.

Hail *Mary!* the refuge of the afflicted Catholicks of *England*.

Hail *Mary!* the powerful protectress of the devout Rosarists of this holy Confraternity.

Hail *Mary!* the solace of the living and the dead.

Be you with us, holy *Mary*, in all the temptations, tribulations, necessities and
infirmities :

infirmities of our life ; and especially affift us in the laft hour of our death ; obtaining then for us a pardon of our fins,
and a happy paffage to our heavenly
Country. *Amen.*

SECTION XII.

JOSEPH:

Or,

Devotions to S. Joseph, *the Glorious
Bridegroom of the Virgin* Mary,
and reputed Father of Chrift Jefus.

The many excellencies, Priviledges,
and Prerogatives of Saint *Joseph*,
are largely deduced by feveral *Learned
Writers:* Out of *whom*, thefe few following are felected, whereupon to
ground our Devotion to this great Saint;
and to lay a foundation for the enfuing
affective Acts, and Elevations.

    1. Saint *Joseph* was fanctified in his
Mothers womb : which favour feems
(in fome fort) due to *him*, who was

have so neer a relation to the Word Incarnate, (the Source and Origin of all
Sanctity) and *who* was design'd from all
Eternity, in the Conclave of the Adorable Trinity, to be the President of Gods
great Council of State upon Earth ; the
Angel Guardian of the Queen of Angels; the reputed Father, and the real
Fosterer, Nurser, Conductor, Gover-
nor of *J E S U S*, the worlds *Messias*,
and the head of his holy Family. Now
since Gods Family consisted only of two
Persons, *Jesus* and *Mary*, who were
of more worth and dignity, than all the
rest of Heavenly and Earthly creatures
together ; it was convenient that *He*,
who was to govern them, should also
resemble them in Greatness, Dignity, and
Sanctity, and consequently that he
should possess in some measure (by an
anticipated pardon of his Original sin,
and by an advanced favour of sanctifying Grace) *that Purity* which the *Son*
possessed by Nature, and the *Mother* by
Priviledge.

2. He was the next after the sacred
Virgin, who made an express Vow and
promise to God, of perpetual Virginity.
And this Resolution , Intention, and
Promise both of *Her*, and *Him*, was re-
veal'd to each other respectively, and

renewed by them jointly, before they
were contracted together by formall
Matrimonie. For how else could Blessed *Mary* (who had oblig'd her self to
virginal Integrity) have consented (either in Prudence or Justice) to give the
Power over her body to a person, of
whose Chastity she might be ignorant, or
doubtful of his Constancy? Surely, the
known purity of her Chast *Bridegroom*,
gave her the confidence to treat and
converse with him, as securely as she did
with the holy Seraphins.

3. He no sooner perceiv'd his Blessed
Spouse to be big with child, but he cast
about how he might handsomly retreat
from her company; not as harbouring
the least doubt or distrust of her Innocency; (being more certain of her Invisible Chastity, than of her visible ap-
pearing to be with child; and knowing that it was more easie for a Virgin
to conceive, than for *Mary* to deceive
him, or distain her own honour); but
out of a deep and humble sense of his
due respect towards her *Son* and her
self; as judging himself altogether unworthy to contemplate with his eyes,
and carry in his arms the Divine Word
Incarnate, and to converse intimately
and familiarly with the glorious Mother

of this God-Man, who was shortly after to be born into the world.

4. He govern'd Gods Family for a-
bove thirty years space. As the Divine
Providence hath establish'd *three* Orders in the world; That of *Nature*, that
of *Grace*, and that of *Hypostatical Union*;
so he hath appointed three sorts of servants for the conduct and government
of these Orders. The *Angels* serve him
in the order of Nature; the *Apostles*
in the order of Grace; but he chose
S. *Joseph* alone (after the sacred Virgin)
to serve him in the third order, which
is that of *Jesus*, in the ineffable Mysterie
of his Incarnation. O the Excellencie,
the Eminencie, the Greatness of Saint
Joseph ! O his honour and happiness, to
enjoy so long the innocent embraces of
Jesus in his Childhood ! The holy entertainments of *Jesus in his riper years* !
The divine actions, examples, and instructions of *Jesus in his perfect age* ! And to
live so long in company and conversation with the most holy and accomplished
Princess that ever was !

5. He (together with his sacred
Spouse) circumcis'd *Jesus*, in the Stable
of *Bethleem*, eight days after his Birth
into the world ; and (according to the
divine order and command, which was

signifi'd unto him by an Angelical Messenger) impos'd upon him that glorious name of JESUS.

6. He nourish'd, fed, and maintained *Him*, with the sweat of his brows, and labour of his hands, *who* affords food and sustenance to all living Creatures. And cloathed *him*, who furnished the Lillies, Roses, and flowers of the Field, with all their beautiful Robes and Ornaments.

7. *He* was (in some sort) the *Saver* of his *Saviour*, by sheltering little *Jesus* from *Herods* rage and cruelty, and stepping aside with him into *Egypt*, whilst the Innocents bought the palm of Martyrdome with the price of their blood.

8. He commanded *him*, who commands all earthly Princes and Monarchs; and had *him* obedient to the beck of his hand, to the nod of his head, to the twinkle of his eye, and to the sound of his voice, before whom the powers of Heaven fall down and tremble. O the admirable power of S. *Joseph!* O the adorable subjection of *Jesus!* O the sublimity of S. *Josephs*, to command *Jesus!* O the Humility of *Jesus*, to obey S. *Joseph*.

9. He possessed and practised all vertues

tues in their perfection; especially *Humility*, as being to pass the remainder of his days in *her* company, *who* being the greatest, was the most humble of all pure creatures; and in *his* company, *who* being the Son of the most high, made himself the least, and lowest amongst the sons of men. Nor can S. *Iosephs* Vertues, Perfections, and Greatnesses, be comprehended and measur'd by any better means than by the greatnesses of *Iesus* and *Mary*, to whom he was so strictly allied; For he was *Mary's* true *Husband*, and consequently the true and legal (though not the carnal and natural) *Father* of *Iesus*. O what communications of affections, what extasies of spirit, what unions of hearts, was there amongst these Three, *I E S U S, M A R I A, I O S E P H*? Now since God gives grace proportionable to each ones place, vocation, and office; surely as S. *Iosephs* Office was exceeding great, so was his grace, vertue, and perfection, great, excellent, and heroique.

10. He was (as the Fathers piously and probably believe) elevated to Heaven, both in Body and Soul, upon the day of his glorious Sons triumphant *Ascension*, and remains there inthron'd next to the Humanity of *Iesus*, and the

Virgin Mary, in the Celestial Kingdom; as he was neareſt and deareſt unto them, during the time of their earthly Pilgrimage,

11. He is the faithful, powerful, and charitable Protector and Advocate of his devout children and clients in the Court of Heaven; as having ſo great credit with his *Son* King *Ieſus*, and his *Spouſe* Queen *Mary*, that his demands may ſeem (in ſome ſort) to be commands, and his petitions being preſented to the Throne of Mercy with a Fathers confidence and authority, will not eaſily be rejected by *Ieſus* in Heaven who was ſo obedient to *Ioſeph* upon Earth.

12. He is the chief Patron of all Contemplatives, and the great Maſter, Guide, and Director, of the Interiour, hidden, and Spiritual life. *S. Tereſa* happily experienc'd this verity; and frequently expreſſed it, ſaying, *They that cannot meet with a Maſter to inſtruct them in the manner of their Prayer; Let them take the Glorious Saint Ioſeph for their Teacher and Tutor, and they ſhall infallibly find the ſafe and ſecure way to ſolid Sanctity and perfection.*

Q

A short Rosary in the honour of S. Jo-
seph: Containing the principal My-
steries of his Life; drawn out of
the precedent Excellencies ; and di-
stinguished into Five Tens, or De-
cades.

Begin also this Rosary, with the sign
of the Cross and the Creed.

The first Decade.

Of his Election.

SAint *IOSEPH* was chosen in
the Council of Gods Eternal Wisdome and Providence, to be the worthy
Bridegroom of *Mary*, and the reputed
Father of *IESUS*.

    Our Father, &c.

  1. He was the highest and the holiest
of the Patriarchs,

      Hail Mary.

  2. He descended from the royal Pro-
geny of *David*.

      Hail Mary.

  3. He was particularly prefigur'd by
Ioseph the deliverer of *Egypt*.

      Hail Mary.   4. He

4. He was sanctifi'd in his Mothers womb.

Hail Mary.

5. He was confirmed in Grace and Vertue.

Hail Mary.

6. He was a just man by the testimony of the Holy Gospel.

Hail Mary.

7. He was instructed from Heaven, in the Mystery of the Incarnation.

Hail Mary.

8. He was indu'd with the plenty of all spiritual blessings.

Hail Mary.

9. He was enriched with gifts and qualities, both natural and supernatural, sutable to the sacred charge, for which he was design'd.

Hail Mary.

10. He was the first, (after the Virgin-Mother) who by Vow consecrated his Virginity to the Divine Majesty.

Hail Mary.

Glory be to the Father, and to the Son, and to the holy Ghost, &c.

The second Decade.

Of his place, office, and dignity.

SAint *Joseph* was appointed the Head, Governour, and Steward, of Gods Family upon Earth.

Our Father, &c.

1. He was espoused to the sacred Virgin *Mary*.

Hail Mary.

2. He was the Guardian and witness of her Virginity; and allotted by Divine Providence to be her Counsellor, Comforter, and Companion, upon all occasions.

Hail Mary.

3. He was her faithful assistant in her journey to *Bethleem*.

Hail Mary.

4. He found out the Stable for her harbour, when the Inns refused to entertain her.

Hail Mary.

5. He was present at our Redeemers happy Birth into the world.

Hail Mary.

6. He help'd the holy Virgin-Mother to swath him, cloath him, and cradle him in the manger.   *Hail Mary.*

7. He was the first, who with the extasi'd Mother, had the honour to adore the New-born Man-God.

Hail Mary.

8. He concurr'd with the sacred Virgin to Chrifts Circumcifion, and together with her, impos'd upon him the fweet Name of *JESUS*.

Hail Mary.

9. He was reverenc'd by the Eaftern Kings, when they offer'd their Royal Prefents to his reputed Son *Iefus*.

Hail Mary.

10. He with his Virgin-Spoufe prefented *IESUS* to his Eternal Father in the Temple.

Hail Mary.

Glory be to the Father, and to the Son, and to the Holy Ghoft, &c.

Thefe Prayers Angelical, &c.

The third Decade

Of his flight into Egypt.

SAint *IOSEPH* took the young Child, and *Mary* his Mother, and departed into *Egypt*; fo preferving *Iefus* from *Herods* cruelty, who fought to opprefs him in his Infancy.

Our Father. &c.

1. He readily, resignedly, and in the night season, obeyed the Angels admonition.

Hail Mary.

2. He cheerfully undertook a long, tedious, and troublesome journey, into an unknown Countrey.

Hail Mary.

3. He patiently endur'd with *Iesus* and *Mary*, a seven years banishment.

Hail Mary.

4. He provided food for him, (with the sweat of his brows, and labour of his hands) who affords food to all living Creatures.

Hail Mary.

5. He cloath'd him, who cloath's the flowers of the field.

Hail Mary.

6. He (next to the sacred Virgin) was the most ardent of all *Iesus*'s lovers; serving him in his exile, with more then Seraphical affection.

Hail Mary.

7. He lov'd the sacred Virgin, with a natural affection, in respect of her eminent perfections: with an acquired affection, in respect of her reciprocal favours; with a supernatural affection, in respect of her celestial dignity.

Hail Mary.

8. He was an Instrumental Coopera-
tor with God, in his great defign of
mans redemption.

Hail Mary.

9. He was (in fome fort) the Saver
of his Saviour, by fheltring him from his
enemies Tyranny.

Hail Mary.

10. His life was a continued Contemplation, Recollection, and Extafie in
the perpetual prefence of Gods Son,
and Gods Mother.

Hail Mary.

*Glory be to the Father, and to the Son,
and to the Holy Ghoft, &c.*

Thefe Prayers Angelical, &c.

The fourth Decade.

*Of his return from Egypt, and of his
Death.*

SAint *I O S E P H* inform'd by Angelical Revelation of *Herods* death,
returns home with *Iefus* and *Mary.*

Our Father, &c.

1. He, *Iefus,* and *Mary,* after their
banifhment, dwell together in *Nazareth.*

Hail Mary.

2. He conducted *Iefus,* when he was

twelve years old, to the Temple in *Ierusalem*.

Hail Mary.

3. He there lost *Iesus* to his unspeakable grief and sorrow.

Hail Mary.

4. He retriv'd him after three days enquiry, sitting amongst the Doctors.

Hail Mary.

5. He reconducts him home to *Nazareth*, where *Iesus* (the great Monarch of both worlds) was subject and obedient to *Iosephs* command.

Hail Mary.

6. And as he had the Priviledge to enjoy the Innocent embraces of *Iesus*, in his childhood, so he had the honour to enjoy his holy entertainments in his riper years; and his divine actions, examples, and instructions in his perfect age. *Hail Mary.*

7. He also had the honour to govern the sacred family of *Iesus* and Mary, for thirty years space.

Hail Mary.

8. He had the happiness to be assisted by *Iesus* and Mary in his last Agony.

Hail Mary.

9. Having compleated the course of his Earthly Pilgrimage, he chang'd this life for Eternity. *Hail Mary.*

10. He sweetly breath'd forth his soul in a high act and sigh of love, in the sacred embraces of *Iesus* and *Mary*.

Hail Mary.

Glory be to the Father, &c.
These Prayers Angelical, &c.

The fifth Decade.

Of his Glory.

SAint *IOSEPH* was elevated to glory upon the day of his Sons triumphant Ascension.

Our Father, &c.

1. He is inthron'd there above, next to *Iesus* and *Mary*; as he was here below neerest and dearest unto them.

Hail Mary.

2. He is adorn'd with a garland of virginity; for having preserv'd it unblemish'd to his last breath.

Hail Mary.

3. He is enobled with the *Aureola* of Doctorship; for having instructed the ignorant, and particularly the Egyptians, in the time of his sojourning amongst them.

Hail Mary.

4. He is rewarded with a Crown

of Martyrdome; for having hazarded his life for his Sons prefervation.

Hail Mary.

5. He is a powerful Protector of all them who are particularly devoted unto him; as having great credit with the All powerful *Iefus.*

Hail Mary.

6. He is the general Patron of the Church Militant, as being the fpecial Favourite of its head *Chrift Iefus.*

Hail Mary.

7. He bears a fingular affection to all that fincerely love *Iefus* and *Mary;* as being fo neerly allied unto them.

Hail Mary.

8. His Petitions are prefented to the Throne of Mercy, with a Fathers confidence; and his Requefts will not eafily be rejected by *Iefus* in heaven, who was fo obedient to *Iofeph* upon earth.

Hail Mary.

9. He is the chief Patron of all Contemplatives.

Hail Mary.

10. He is the great Mafter, Guide, and Director, of the Interiour, hidden, and fpiritual life.

Hail Mary.

Glory be to the Father, and to the Son, and to the Holy Ghoft, &c.

These Prayers Angelical with bended knees, &c.

Credo, &c. as in the great Rosary of the Blessed Virgin Mary.

Conclude this Rosary with the ensuing Oblation.

An Oblation to

St. IOSEPH:

To honour God in him, and him in God, in his Dignity of being the reputed FATHER of the Word Incarnate, and the BRIDEGROOM of the Blessed Virgin MARIE.

And to offer up our selves to him, in the state of dependency, which is due to him upon these titles; and to correspond by our inward devotion to that power which he hath over us, by consequence of the power he had over the Son and Mother of GOD.

GReat and glorious Patriarch, St. Joseph! The worthy Bridegroom of *Mary*, and esteemed *Father* of *Jesus*! In the honour of Gods beholding and electing you in the Council of his Eternal Wisdom; and of his placing you, at the time appointed by his divine Providence, *in these two* high and sublime estates.

In honour and union of all the singular graces, prerogatives, priviledges, and perfections, which he plentifullie heap'd upon you, in order to render you capable of these eminent offices, and undertakings.

In honour and union of your souls extraordinarie Sanctitie, of your Bodies Virginal Puritie, of your profound Humilitie, of your perfect Obedience, of your voluntarie Povertie, and of all the rest of your consummated vertues.

In honour and union of your dear affection to *Jesus*, and *Mary*, of the continual application of your spirit towards these two divine objects; of the tenderness of your devotion unto them, and of your silent, solitarie, retired, recollected, and contemplative life with them.

In honour and union of all the services, you rendred to the Word Incarnate, in the state and order of his hypostatical union with our Nature.

In honour and union of that last Act and sigh of love, wherein you sweetlie breathed forth your faithful soul in the embraces of *Jesus* and *Mary*, your divine Son, and dear Spouse.

In honour, homage, and union of all your other Greatnesses, and especiallie of the right, power, and jurisdiction you had over *Jesus* and *Mary* in quality of *Father* and *Husband*, and of the subjection, obedience, and dutie they rendred you.

Finallie, in acknowledgment of your having been established the Head, the Steward, and the Director of Gods Familie upon Earth ; The Father, the Tutor, and the Trainer up of *Jesus*; the Bridegroom, the Guardian, and the Helper of the holie Virgin *Mary*.

I do now choose you (O great and glorious Patriarch !) for my particular Patron, for my pious Father, and for my chief Director, next after *Jesus* and *Mary*.

And upon this score, I do here yield and resign unto you all the power I have over my self ; willing to submit my self to you, as my Saviour Jesus was subject unto you : and begging your leave, to place (next after *Jesus* and *Mary*) all the future transactions, motions, and passages of my life, during this my
earthlie

earthlie pilgrimage, under your sacred conduct, government, and protection.

Make me worthy, (O glorious Father!) by your merits, to become (with you) a faithful Member of the Familie of *Jesus* and *Mary*; and to be thereunto firmlie and intimatelie united, associated, and incorporated by Grace and Sanctitie: and obtain for me by your powerful intercession, that I may never be separated from sweet *Jesus* and *Mary*, in my Life, in my Death, in my Eternitie.

Take also (O powerful Patron!) the last moment of my life, (that moment which must decide my Eternitie,) into your pious care and custodie: Assist me then, I beseech you, in that harsh passage; and obtain for me a happie death and departure out of this World, in the faith, favour, and affection of *Jesus*: To whom be all honour, praise, and glory for evermore. *Amen.*

Litania de Sancto Iosepho, quæ in Processione, in Festo ipsius, in Capella sancti Rosarii recitantur.

Antiphona.

Salve Joseph sanctissime,
Patriarcharum maxime,
Ecclesiæ Oeconome,
Mariæ custos fidele,
Christique Pater inclite!
   Kyrie eleison.
   Christe eleison.
   Kyrie eleison.
   Christe audi nos.
Christe exaudi nos.
Pater de cœlis Deus
Fili Redemptor mundi Deus } Miserere
Spiritus sancte Deus nobis.
Sancta Trinitas unus Deus,
Sancta Maria, Beati Josephi Sponsa castissima

Sancte Joseph {
Advocate humillime.
Benedicte in hominibus.
Confirmate in gratia.
Defensor pauperum & innocentium
Exul cum Christo in Egypto
Favorita Regis Cælestis
} Ora pro nobis.

Guardiane Verbi Incarnati,

Honorabilis coram Deo & hominibus,

Idea & exemplar omnium virtutum,

Lilium puritatis,

Miraculum castitatis,

Nutricie Dei Filii,

Obsequentissime serve Iesu & Mariæ,

Patrone contemplativorum,

Quintessentia perfectionis,

Regulator Familiæ Iesu Christi,

Spiritualis Director vitæ internæ,

Tutor doctorque animarum ad cælum aspirantium,

Vniuersalis Advocate & Intercessor pro Ecclesia militante,

Sanctæ Ioseph, *Ora pro nobis.*

Agnus Dei, qui tollis peccata mundi,
  Parce nobis Domine.
Agnus Dei, qui tollis peccata mundi,
  Exaudi nos Domine.
Agnus Dei qui tollis peccata mundi,
  Miserere nobis.
Versi. Ora pro nobis beatissime Ioseph!
Resp. Vt digni efficiamur promissionibus Christi.

Oremus.

SAnctissimæ Genetricis tuæ Sponsi, quæsumus Domine, meritis adjuuemur ; ut *quod possibilitas nostra non obtinet, ejus nobis intercessione donetur. Qui vivis & regnas cum Deo Patre, in unitate Spiritus sancti Deus, Per omnia secula seculorum. Amen.*

The Litanies of St. Joseph, which are recited in the Procession, made upon his Feast, in the Chappel of the holy Rosary.

The Anthem.

ALL hail holy Joseph,
Chief of the Patriarchs,
Steward of Gods Church,
Faithful Preserver of the Virgin *Mary*,
And renowned Father of Christ Jesus.

 Lord have mercy upon us.
 Christ have mercy upon us.
 Lord have mercy upon us.
 Christ hear us.
O Christ graciously hear us,
O God the Father, Creator of the World,
O God the Son, Redeemer of Mankind,
O God the Holy Ghost, Perfecter of the Elect,
Holy Trinitie, one God,

Holy *Mary*, the chaste Spouse of *Jo-seph*,

Advocate of the humble,
Blessed amongst men,
Confirmed in grace,
Defender of the Poor and In-nocent,
Exiled with Christ into Egypt,
Favourite of the King of Hea-ven,
Guardian of the Word Incar-nate,
Honourable before God and Men,
Idea and exemplar of all vertue
Lillie of Puritie,
Miracle of Chastitie,
Nursing Father to Gods Son,
Obsequious servant to *Jesus* and *Mary*,
Patron of Contemplatives,
Quintessence of perfection,
Ruler of the Familie of *Jesus*,
Spirituall Director of the inte-riour life,
Teacher and tutor of souls aspiring to Heaven,
Universal Intercessor for the Church militant,

Holy Ioseph.

Pray for us.

Lamb of God, who takest away the sins
of the World,

Spare us O Lord.

Lamb of God, who takest away the sins
of the World.

Hear us, O Lord.

Lamb of God, who takest away the sins
of the World,

Have mercy upon us.

Ver. Pray for us O most blessed
Joseph.

Ans. That we may be made worthy
of Christ's Promises.

Let us pray.

ASsist us, O Lord I we beseech you,
by the merits of St. *Joseph,* your sacred Mothers Bridegroom; that what
we are unworthy to obtain, may be
granted us by his intercession: Who
livest and reignest, with the Father, in
unitie of the Holy Ghost, one God for
evermore. *Amen.*

*A Devout Prayer to S. Joseph, to implore
his particular protection and direction.*

O Glorious Patriark, the faithful Steward of Gods Familie, and worthy
Guardian of *Jesus* and *Mary!* powring
here forth my soul before you, I most

humbly implore your holy patronage,
protection and direction,for the discreet
managing of this my whole lives remaining pilgrimage. I beg no other favour
of you, (*O great Favourite of King Jesu!*) but only to obtain such gifts and
graces for me, as may render me agrea-
ble to my divine Saviour. Yet if I may
be permitted to particularize my wants,
and determinate my wishes: I most in-
stantlie crave your assistance (*O great
Master of perfection!*) in my combate
against such a passion, which continuallie
persecutes me; in the rooting out of
such and such a Vice, which perpetually
tempts me; in the cancelling of such and
such an evil custome, which incessantlie
inslaves me; in the breaking of such fetters, affections, condescensions, which
miserably engage me to creatures, and
much hinder my intended and desired
-adhesion to my Creator,according to my
duty and obligation. Give me leave al-
so(*O glorious Saint!*)to put all the days,
hours, and minutes of my life, under
your particular protection and powerful safeguard; and especially that last moment whereupon depends my eternity.

SECTION XIII.

THE
Devout Association
OF THE
PIOUS ROSARISTS.
In the

Oratory of the ever
Blessed Virgin *MARY*
of Power and of
Suffrages:

For the charitable relief
and assistance of the
Souls suffering in
PURGATORY.

*According to the special grant and appro-
bation of Pope* Alexander VII. *now sitting;* [*as appears by his Brief, dated
on the* 1. *of* March, 1659. *in the fifth
year of his Popedom.*]
The Preface.

Though Prayers and Suffrages for
departed Souls, were perpetually in

use in the Catholick Church; (as might
be most plainly and particularlie instan-
ced, by producing the Authorities and
Practises of the Holy Fathers and Doctors in all Ages, from the Apostles
daies to this present) Yet the first *Association* and Confederation of certain
more devout Christians, who agreed
together in this most charitable design,
and who obliged themselves to perform
several particular Acts of Piety for the
departed Members of their own Fellowship; seems to have begun in the
year of our Redeemer 984. as *Baronius*
relates in these express terms:

IN this Year 984. was contracted a
Home an Association and Fellowship
of many Priests, amongst whom were also
some Bishops, to this end and purpose: That
each on of them might be relieved after
their Death, by the Sacrifices of their fel-
low-Brethren.

The Institution hereof is yet extant
in the *Diaconia* of the holy Martyrs
Cosmas and *Damianus*, where in a
Marble Table, remains this engraved
Monument:

Bishops and our Successors for ever, do stand engaged by the solemn Promise, which we sincerely made in the presence of God and his Saints, to say forty Masses for the Souls of such of our Confraternity, as shall pass out of this life before us: Yet so, as that if any shall be hindred by infirmity, such an omission shall not be imputed to him for a sin: But if he recovers his former health, he is obliged to perform his former obligation, &c. And this promise was made before the sacred Altar of God in this Hall, in the time of Pope John 14. on the 22. day of February, in the 12th Indiction, in the year of our Lords Incarnation, 984.

The same pious *Association* is kept on foot and revived in many Cities of *Italy*, in order to help the Souls of the departed by holy and devout Suffrages: And one day of each Week is deputed to this purpose, in which they cloath the *Churches* and *Altars* with mourning, as upon the day it self of the solemn Commemoration of the Dead; singing the Office, and saying a solemn Mass for them; as also applying all the rest of the private *Masses* there celebrated on that day, for the relief of the departed members of their Association: Multitudes of there together, to pour forth their prayers, to obtain Indulgences, and to distribute their Alms; having for this end a *B O X* appointed with this Inscription: *THE BOX OF ALMS FOR THE RELIEF OF SOULS IN PURGATORY.*

THey have moreover certain *Orders*, *Laws* and *Rules*, agreed on to be observed by the Brethren and Sisters of their Association: And they name *Deputies*, who take care to see the Alms, Legacies, and other charitable Distributions satisfied according to the Donor's intention.

At *Rome* especially (the head City of the whole world,) an *Arch-confraternity of Suffrages* chiefly flourisheth; which is therefore so called, because it hath the prime place and preeminence above all the rest of these Associations, which are instituted for the succour of Souls suffering in Purgatory. Into this many of the *Roman Nobility* are inscribed; The most eminent *Cardinals* are its Protectors; and the most illustrious *Lords* are its immediate Governours and Directors; conceiving it a singular honour to take upon them the charge of so renowned a Company.

And to shew the solidity of this sort of Devotion, we shall need only to produce the *Apostolical* Authority: For besides *that* above mentioned Confraternity, begun at *Rome* in the year 984. Pope *Clement* the eighth (in the year 1594.) instituted likewise in the City, an Arch-confraternity of *Suffrages* for the souls in Purgatory; and others of his successors have confirmed the same: To which many Confraternities of like nature were since annexed; and more may be yet aggregated through the whole world, wheresoever the peoples piety excites them to so charitable an enterprise.

Now, since all the *Indulgences* granted *to the living Members of the holy Rosary, may be applied for the dead*; it follows, that the *Indulgences of the Stations of Rome*, and all other City-Indulgences and Priviledges granted to this our Arch-confraternity of the sacred *Rosary*, may also relieve the poor Souls suffering in Purgatory; and that the devout *Rosarists* may every day free some plenary *Indulgence*, and *the delivery of a Soul* out of Purgatory, is annexed to the due performance of these Acts of Piety. *Toties quoties*, how oft soever they are done, without any restriction. And it appears in our greater *Rosary Book*, (entituled *Jesus, Maria, Joseph, S. 13. num. 11. and 12.) that there is *every day* in one part or other of the City, the *Delivery of a Soul* out of Purgatory: And in the Church of S. *John Lateran*, a Plenary may be gained *six times* every day. All which and other City-Indulgences, are expresly granted to all the Brothers and Sisters of the sacred *Rosary*, (performing the aforesaid Devotions) by Pope *Leo* X. in the year 1518. at the instance of the Fathers of the Order of the Preachers, gathered together in that year at *Rome*, in their general Chapter; in his Brief, beginning, *Etsi temporalium cura, &c.* and confirmed by the succeeding chief Pastors. *Indulgences* (says *Carthagena* [*]) so *Great*, that no one can desire greater; and so *certain* and *approved*, that no one can wish more certainty and approbation.

[* *l. 16. hom. 6. in Fest. Rosarii.*]

Wherefore as *We* the faithful members of the Arch-confraternity of the

holy *Rosary,* have hitherto endeavoured
(and shall through Gods grace and assistance continue our endeavours) to gain
Indulgences for the living : So also, (in
imitation of these before-mentioned
pious, zealous, and heroick Spirits intending to make the best use we can of
the vast treasure of Indulgences granted
to our said Arch-confraternity ; We re-
solve to put in practise (in this our
Head-Oratory of the sacred Virgin-Mother of Power and of suffrages for the
Dead,) the pious Exercises, prescribed
in the following *Rules* of this our Association, for the relief of the *Souls suffering in Purgatory.*

Not doubting, but that many of our
more zealous fellow-members of the
Rosary, will joyfully desire to become
our *Associats* in so charitable an Insti-
tute, and our Co-adjutors in so pious
an enterprise ; for the increase of Gods
honour, the good of their own souls,
and the comfort of them departed ;
which are the sole ends we aim at in
this our pious *Association,* under the
Laws, Priviledges, Prerogatives, of the
Arch-confraternity of the sacred *Rosary.*

And surely, if it is conceived an action
praise-worthy, convenient, and necessary, to establish *Schools, Confraternities,*

Hospitals, in all Towns, Cities, and Countries, for the solace of the poor, and for the succour of such persons, as are fallen into extreme penury, misery, and calamity: How much more convenient, christian, and charitable a work is it, to erect *Associations of Suffrages* for the relief of such poor souls, as ly burning in Purgatory without being consumed; and which incessantly cry out unto us, from those caverns of their extreme calamity: *Pity us, O you our compassionate Friends! pity us; for the severe hand of the Divine Justice, lies heavy upon us; nor can we help our selves here, (as you may, who are there yet living) or hope for a cessation of our sufferings, but by the charitable means of your suffrages.*

O Father of Mercies, and Fountain of all Goodness! Inspire from above the hearts of all Christians, to promote every where this great and singular work of Piety towards these poor Souls suffering in Purgatory. Thrice happy they, (says a grave and learned *Writer*,) and worthy eternal memory, praise, and be-

Alms distributed, not only for the *Poor yet living*, but for the *Poor departed*. Surely such heroick persons, may expect high rewards for such holy works of charity. For if (as the Prophet *Daniel* affirms) *They shall shine like stars in the Firmament of perpetual eternity, who shall teach many to justice*; what may we not affirm of them, who shall shew mercy to a whole multitude, and by whose charitable means these millions of miserably afflicted Souls in Purgatory, shall be freed from their punishments, and seated in the happy mansions of an eternal Kingdome! No humane Tongue is capable to express the height of that Glory, which these Souls gain by such charitable endeavours, nor consequently the height of their merit, who shall procure it: *Merit*, which will receive a continual encrease, till the worlds final consummation.

And now let us set down a compendious draught of such *Lawes*, *Rules*, and *Orders*, whereby this our now happily begun *Association* of Suffrages for the Dead, may be hereafter governed and directed.

Rules and Laws, for the Direction and Government of this Association of Suffrages for the Dead.

I.

SInce *Faith* is the foundation of Prayer, (as the Apostle expresly tels us) *He that comes to God must believe ;*) for it purifies our hearts, espouses our souls to God, causes our Prayer to be heard, and our Petitions granted : Therefore, Upon the day that any one is first received and inroll'd into this devout Association : He shall make a *Profession of his Faith*, before the Head Altar of the Virgin-Mother of Power and of Suffrages, in the ample manner and form following.

The profession of Faith.

I (*A. B.*) *do believe in one God, the Father Almighty, Maker of heaven and Earth, of all things visible and invisible:*

by whom all things were made: Who for us men, and for our salvation, descended from Heaven, and was incarnated by the Holy Ghost, of the Virgin Mary; And was made Man. Was also crucified for us under Pontius Pilate, Suffered, Dyed, and was Buried. And he arose on the third day according to the Scriptures: and ascended into Heaven, and sits at the right hand of the Father. And is to come again with glory to judge the Living and the Dead; of whose Kingdome there shall be no end. And in the Holy Ghost the Lord & Life-giver; who proceeds from the father and the Son; and together with the Father and the Son is Adored and Glorified; who spake by the Prophets. And I believe One, Holy, Catholick and Apostolick Church. I confess one Baptism for Remission of sins: And I expect the Resurrection of the Dead; and the Life of the World to come.

I do stedfastly admit and embrace Apostolical and Ecclesiastical Traditions; and the other Observances and Constitutions of the Church.

Also I admit the holy Scripture according to that sense, which our holy Mother the Church, to whom it belongs to judge of the true sense and interpretation of the holy Scriptures, hath held and doth hold: Neither will I ever take and interpret it otherwise than according to the unanimous consent of the Fathers.

I do also profess that there are truly and properly Seven Sacraments of the new Law, instituted by our Lord Jesus Christ, and necessary for the salvation of mankind, though they are not all necessary for every man: That is to say, Baptism, Confirmation, the Eucharist, Penance, Extreme Unction, Order, and Matrimony: And that they do confer Grace: And that of these, Baptism, Confirmation and Order, cannot be re-iterated without Sacriledge.

Also I receive and admit the received and approved Rites of the Catholick Church, in the solemn administration of the aforesaid Sacraments.

Also I embrace and receive all and every the things which are defined and declared in the holy Council of Trent, concerning Original Sin and Justification.

I profess also, That in the Mass there is offered unto God a true, proper, and propitiatory Sacrifice for the living and the dead; And that in the most holy Sacrament of the Eucharist, there is truly, really, and substantially, the Body and Blood, together with the Soul and Divinity of our Lord Jesus Christ; And that there is made a Conversion of the whole substance of the Bread into the Body, and of the whole substance of the Wine into the Blood: Which Conversion the Catholick Church calleth Transubstantiation.

I confess also, that under either sole Species, all and whole Christ, and a true Sacrament is received.

I do constantly hold, that there is a Purgatory, and that the Souls therein detained, are helped by the suffrages of the faithfull.

Likewise, That the Saints reigning with Christ, are to be worshipped and prayed unto; And that they offer Prayers to God for us; And that their Reliques are to be honoured.

I most firmly avouch, That the Images of Christ, and of the Mother of God the perpetual Virgin, and of other Saints also, are to be had and retained; and that due honour and veneration is to be given them.

Also, I affirm, That the power of Indulgences was left by Christ in the Church; And that the use of them, is most wholesome to Christian people.

I acknowledge the holy Catholick and Apostolick Roman Church, for the Mother and Mistrifs of all Churches; and I promise and swear true Obedience to the Bishop of Rome, successor to St. Peter, Prince of the Apostles, and Vicar of Christ.

I do likewife undoubtedly receive and profess all other things delivered, defined, and declared by the facred Canons and Councils of the Oecumenical, and particularly by the holy Council of Trent : *And withall, I do condemn, Reject, and Anathematize, all things which are contrary thereunto ; and all Herefies whatfoever which the Church hath condemned, rejected and anathematized.*

And I do promife, vow, and fwear, That I will be careful to hold and conftantly confefs (through Gods help and affiftance) this true Catholick Faith, out of which no man can be faved : Which at this prefent I do willingly profefs, and truly hold : And alfo, That I fhall endeavour (as far forth as I am able) to have the fame held, taught and profeffed by thofe who are under me, or over whom, by reafon of my charge, I fhall have care, power, and authority.

So help me God, and all his holy Saints.

2.

Whofoever will become a Member of this pious *Affociation*, whether Man or Woman) to the end he may begin his Exercifes with a pure and upright intention, to the encreafe of Gods glory, his own merit, and the comfort of the fouls in Purgatory ; fhall upon the day of his entrance, endeavour to cleer his conscience by *Sacramental Confession*; or at least, by producing (as much as in him lies) an Act of *sincere Contrition:* This surely, as it is a most profitable practise for all Christians; so it is chiefly to be recommended to the frequent use of the Brothers and Sisters of the Arch-confraternity of the sacred *Rosary,* and to the members of this pious *Association* of Suffrages; whom it behoves to be always so disposed and prepared, as that they should be evermore found fit and ready to receive the Sacraments. For Indulgences are not indifferently obtain'd by all sorts of persons; but by such only as have duly and diligently purified, prepared, and disposed their souls to receive them, by precedent Penance, &c. (as is more at large declared in our Rosary Book, §. 12.)

Upon the same day also of his entrance; (or, if then lawfully hindered at his next opportunity); he shall receive the *Blessed Sacrament,* applying the fruit of his Communion to the faithful departed.

3.

Every day throughout the whole year, *The Stations of Rome* shall be performed in the Oratory of the Blessed Virgin *Mary*, of Power, and of Suffrages, for the benefit of the Souls suffering in Purgatory, (as they are practically set down in the next following Section.)

Also, The *Office of the Dead*, shall be there recited, upon each first Monday of the Month, and upon each Monday in Advent and Lent, according to the Rubricks of the Roman Breviary.

4.

Four *Anniversaries* shall be celebrated every year at the Rosary Altar, for the Souls of all our departed Brethren and Sisters, upon the Morrows of the four principal Feasts of our Blessed Virgin-Mother, which are these; *Her Nativity, her Annunciation, her Purification, her Assumption:* At which times the Rosarists (not otherwise hindered) should also assist, that they may expect the same Piety from their surviving Brethren, after their own departure. And during the celebration of these Anniversaries, they are not sleightly but seriously to remember their deceased Brethren and Sisters of this *Confraternity,* and more particularly them of this *Association*; recommending their Souls to God the Father, through Jesus Christ our Redemer and Mediatour : And this chiefly after the *Elevation* of the sacred Eucharist, when the Priest, in the name of the whole Church, makes a memoriall of all the faithful departed.

5.

Upon each first Monday of every Month, (not hindered by some solemn Feast of the Church) shall be celebrated at the Head Altar, a *solemn Mass of Requiem*, which shall be particularly applied to the faithful members departed of this Confraternity and Association : And the grace and Indulgence of the Priviledg'd Altar, shall be applied to that Soul, which (amongst them) is in greatest need thereof : And upon the same day shall be made a *Procession* (either before or after the chief Mass) for the same intention : In which the Litanies for the faithful departed, shall be recited ; together with such Prayers as are hereafter set down.

6.

The Members of this Association, shall dayly recite the Psalm *De profundis* with the Versicle and Collect : Or the illiterate shall say *three Paters and Aves* for the departed Brethren and Sisters of this

7.

As often as it shall please God to call any member of this Association out of the World: All the Brethren and Sisters thereof, shall once at their first opportunitie be present at *Mass* to pray for his Soul, or shall recite the *Office of the Dead* for him, or the *Seven Penitential Psalmes*, or the whole *Rosary* of the sacred Virgin. [For as often as any Rosarist (being duly disposed for the gaining of Indulgencies) shall recite the whole Rosary for the Souls departed, he gaines a Soul out of Purgatory, (as is declared in our larger *Rosary* Book. §. 13. *Numb.* 9.]

8.

A Mass of *Requiem* shall solemnlie be celebrated in the head Oratorie, for each member newlie departed of this Association ; with an application of the Priviledge above mentioned. It belongs therefore to the care of the Friends of the departed Brother or Sister, to signifie speedilie the day of their death to one of the Treasurers, appointed for that purpose ; who with like speed and diligence shall signifie the same to the rest of his Fellow-members, (at least, fo many of them, as he can conveniently fummon ;) to the end they may be prefent at the celebration of thefe Funerals, upon the day defigned by the Spiritual Director, and fignified to them by the faid Treafurer.

9.

A Book fhall be appointed, wherein the Day of each Brothers and Sifters Departure, fhall be punctuallie *regiftred,* (together with what Alms they bequeath to pious ufes for the good of their Souls,) by the Secretary of the Affociation : to the end there may be a perpetual memorial of their Charitie; and that they may be *annually* prayed for, by their furviving Brethren and Sifters.

10.

Every Year, an *Octave* fhall be deputed for the fuccour of the Souls in Purgatorie; to wit, From the day of the Commemoration of all Souls untill the Eighth day following: In which *Octave* a Solemn *Mafs of Requiem* fhall be dayly celebrated at the Head-Altar; with an intention of helping chiefly thofe Souls, which have longeft remained in the punifhments of Purgatory : And the grace and favour of the Priviledged Altar fhall be particularly applied to that departed Soul of this *Affociation*, which fhall ftand in greateft need thereof.

II.

They who are more zealous and fervent in praying for the faithful departed, and who by a laudable cuftome come frequently to the facred Communion; fhall do very pioufly to offer up that propitiatory Sacrifice for the Soul of the lately departed member of this Affociation, and to apply their Communion for his relief and comfort.

When therefore their Charity towards their departed friends fhall excite them to this efficacious fort of Devotion: Let them entertain themfelves during that whole day (fet apart for that holy purpofe,) in fuch Acts, Exercifes, and Cogitations, as are proper for that fubject; according to the Practical method, prefcribed in our Book of the *Chriftians daily Exercife,* § 18. They may alfo moft laudably add works of Super-erogation, as Alms, Penances Mortifications, and fuch other Acts of Mercy and Piety, as their own private Devotion fhall fuggeft unto them: Which when they have faithfullie, ferventlie, and with a pure intention performed; they may hopefully expect the happy accomplishment of their Redeemers firm promise, made to them in the holy Gospel, *Mat. 5. Blessed are the merciful, for they shall obtain Mercy.*

12.

As for the Government of this our *Association* of Suffrages for the Dead: We conceive it sufficient for the present, (the times, and circumstances duly considered,) To make choice of *one worthy Patron* or Protector, who, whilst he lives, shall remain in that Office: Of *two Spiritual Directors,* who are to see these Prayers, Exercises, and Devotions for the Dead, dayly and punctually performed at the head-Altar: Of *two Treasurers,* who are to take care of the Alms, and of all things necessary for the maintenance and ornament of the said Altar: And lastly, Of *a Secretary,* who is to take the Names of such zealous persons as desire to be admitted and inrolled into this sacred Association.

13.

The Officers aforesaid of this Association, may either wear a *Ring* with a *Deaths-head* engraved upon it; or something elfe, which may be hereafter agreed upon amongft themfelves, to be born by them, as a particular badge of their piety towards the Souls in Purgatory.

14.

Finally, though all thefe Laws, Orders, and Rules, are in themfelves very pious and profitable; and the Acts thereby prefcribed, (being performed with a pure, fimple, fincere, and charitable intention,) are very meritorious to them who fhall pleafe to aggregate themfelves together in fo holy an Affociation: Yet let them reft fecure, That none of them are intended *to tye their Confciences*, or to oblige them under the pain of any fin, to the practice thereof; but only, That they are for that time deprived of the merit of all fuch works, as they fhall then neglect or omit to put in execution.

The Conclufion.

AND now (moft Honoured and devout *Rofarifts!*, let us ferioufly reflect back our thoughts upon the greatnefs and goodnefs of this pious defign of erecting here amongft us this holy

Association of Suffrages for the relief of the Souls in Purgatory: An *Association* of so singular Charity towards them, and of so much Benefit to our selves: whereby *they* shall be made partakers of so many Suffrages, Sacrifices, Prayers, Alms-deeds, and other devout Actions, and *we* of so great Priviledges and Indulgences. Surely no day will pass, in which some Soul will not be freed from her punishment by these our pious endeavours; and in which we shall not by the same means encrease our own merit.

For can we doubt, but that they coming to their Kingdom, will be mindful of them who wrought their felicity, and procured their speedy release from their dismal Banishment? Will not so many of them, as have received solace by our Suffrages, become our Advocates and Patrons? Will they not reciprocally pray for us, and plead our cause at the Tribunal of Gods *Mercy*; since we pleaded theirs so charitably at the Tribunal of his *Justice*? Will they not ob-

ly intone the Canticles of divine praises
for all Eternity?

Let us therefore (whom the preve-
nient Grace of God, from whom all
good proceeds, hath inspired with these
pious intentions, of assisting the poor
Souls suffering in Purgatory to the ut-
most of our power ;) joyntly endeavour
the settlement, promotion, and propa-
gation of this charitable *Association* :
And so much the rather at this time,
when some new-Divines endeavour to
broach certain Doctrines, which seem
very much to derogate from this ancient and authentick sort of Devotion
and Piety.

Litania pro fidelibus defunctis.

KYrie eleison.
Christe eleison.
Kyrie eleison.
Christe audi nos.
Christe exaudi nos.
Pater de cœlis Deus,
    Miserere omnium fidelium defuncto-
rum.

Fili Redemptor mundi Deus,
    Miserere omnium fidelium defunctorū.
Spiritus Sancte Deus,
    Miserere omnium fidelium defunctorū.
Sancta Maria,
Sancta Dei Genitrix,
Sancta Virgo Virginum,
Sancte Michael,
Omnes sancti Angeli & Archangeli,
Sancte Joannes Baptista,
S. Petre,
S. Paule,
S. Joannes,
Omnes sancti Apostoli & Evangelista,
S. Stephane,
S. Laurenti,
Omnes sancti Martyres,
S. Gregori,
S. Ambrosi,
Omnes sancti Pontifices & Confesso-
    res,
Sancta Maria Magdalena,
Sancta Catharina,
Omnes sancta Virgines & Vidua,
Omnes sancti & sancta Dei, Intercedite
    pro fidelibus defunctis.
Propitius esto. Parce eis Domine.
Propitius esto. Exaudi eos Domine.
Ab omni malo. Libera eos Domine.

Orate & orate pro fidelibus defunctis.

Ab ira tua,

A potestate Diaboli,

A flamma ignis,

A Regione umbra mortis,

Per immacula: ā Conceptionem tuam

Per Natiuitatem & Circumcisionem
　　tuam,

Per acerbissimam Passionem tuam,

Per sanctissima vulnera tua

Per pretiosissimum sanguinem tuum,

Per crudelissimam & ignominiosissi-
　　mam mortem tuam,

Per multitudinem miserationum tu-
　　arum,

Peccatores, Te rogamus audi nos.

Qui Mariam absoluisti & Latronem
　　exaudisti.

Ut parentes propinquos & benefacto-
　　res nostros a pœnis inferni eripere
　　digneris,

Ut omnes fideles defunctos, ab aterna
　　damnatione liberare digneris,

Ut desiderium ipsorum adimplere dig-
　　neris,

Ut Angelorum cœtus eis subueniat,

Ut eis Patriarcharum & Propheta-
　　rum cunctus occurrat,

Ut eos gloriosus Apostolorum chorus
　　excipiat,

Ut candidatorum Martyrum trium-
　　phans exercitus eos latus circumdet,

Libera eos Domine.

Te rogamus audi nos.

Ut eos sanctorum Confessorum agmen
   deducat,

Ut jubilantium Virginum eos corona
   comitetur,

Ut, mitis atq́; dulcis Jesu! tuus eis
   aspectus benignus appareat,

Ut ad dexteram tuam in electorum
   consortium eos recipias,

Ut eorum fidelium defunctorum quo-
   rum specialis in terra memoria non
   habetur, misereri digneris,

Ut fratres ac sorores, ex hac nostra
   confraternitate & Associatione de-
   functos a pænis Purgatorii eripere
   digneris,

Fili Dei! Fons pietatis,

Fili Dei! Rex Majestatis,

Te rogamus audi nos.

Agnus Dei! qui tollis peccata mundi,
   Dona eis requiem.

Agnus Dei! qui tollis peccata mundi,
   Dona eis requiem.

Agnus Dei! qui tollis peccata mundi,
   Dona eis requiem sempiternam.

Christe audi nos.

Christe exaudi nos.

   Pater noster, &c.

   Versic. Et ne nos inducas in tentationem.

   Resp. Sed libera nos à malo.

   Versic. Requiem eternam dona eis Do-
mine.

   Resp. Et lux perpetua luceat eis.

Verf. *A porta inferi.*

Resp. *Libera Domine animas eorum.*

Verf. *Requiescant in pace.*

Resp. *Amen.*

Verf. *Domine exaudi orationem meam.*

Resp. *Et clamor meus ad te veniat.*

Verf. *Dominus vobiscum.*

Resp. *Et cum Spiritu tuo.*

Oremus.

1. *In die obitus, sive Anniversarii.*

DEus cui proprium est misereri semper & parcere: te supplices exoramus pro anima famuli tui N. quam de hoc saeculo migrare jussisti: ut non tradas eam in manus inimici, neq, obliviscaris in finem sed jubeas eam a sanctis Angelis suscipi, & ad patriam Paradisi perduci: ut quia in te speravit & credidit, non poenas inferni sustineas, sed gaudia sempiterna possideat. Per Christum Dominum nostrum.

Resp. *Amen.*

2. *Pro omnibus fidelibus defunctis.*

FIdelium Deus omnium conditor & redemptor, animabus famulorum famularumque tuarum remissionem cunctorum hac peccatorum: ut indulgentiam quam *semper optaverunt, piis supplicationibus consequantur. Qui vivis & regnas in sæcula seculorum.*

Resp. *Amen.*

3. Pro Fratribus, Affinibus & Benefactoribus.

DEus venia largitor, & humanæ salutis amator; quæsumus clementiam tuam, ut nostræ Congregationis fratres, propinquos & benefactores, qui ex hoc sæculo transierunt; beata Maria semper Virgine intercedente cum omnibus sanctis tuis, ad perpetua beatitudinis consortium pervenire concedas. Per Dominum, &c.

Resp. *Amen.*

Modus officiandi pro mortuis.

Sacerdos aspergit feretrum aqua benedicta, dicens:

Antiphona.

SI iniquitates observaveris Domine; Domine quis sustinebit?

Deinde recitat, *Psalmum,* 129.

De profundis clamavi ad te Domine; Domine exaudi vocem meam:

Fiant aures tuæ intendentes: in vocem deprecationis meæ.

Si iniquitates observaveris Domine: Domine! quis sustinebit?

Quia apud te propitiatio est: & propter legem tuam sustinui te Domine.

Sustinuit anima mea in verbo ejus: speravit anima mea in Domino.

A custodia matutina usque ad noctem, speret Israel in Domino.

Quia apud Dominum misericordia, & copiosa apud eum redemptio.

Et ipse redimet Israel; ex omnibus iniquitatibus ejus.

Vers. *Requiem eternam dona eis Domine.*

Resp. *Et lux perpetua luceat eis.*

Primum Responsorium.

Subvenite Sancti Dei, occurrite Angeli Domini; Suscipientes animam ejus, & offerentes eam in conspectu Altissimi.

Vers. *Suscipiat te Christus, qui vocavit te; & in sinum Abrahæ Angeli deducant te.*

Et repetitur.

Suscipientes animam ejus, & offerentes eam in conspectu Altissimi.

Vers. *Requiem æternam dona eis Domine.*

Resp. *Et lux perpetua luceat eis.*

Offerentes eam in conspectu Altissimi.

Pater noster, &c.   Secreto..

Verf. Et ne nos inducas in tentationem.

Refp. Sed libera nos a malo.

Verf. A porta inferi.

Refp. Erue Domine animam ejus.

Verf. Requiefcat in pace.

Refp. Amen.

Verf. Domine exaudi orationem meam.

Refp. Et clamor meus ad te veniat.

Verf. Dominus vobifcum.

Refp. Et cum Spiritu tuo.

Oremus.

ABfolve quæfumus, Domine, animam famuli tui, [vel famula, vel famulorum, &c.] ab omni vinculo delictorum, ut in Refurrectionis gloria inter fanctos & electos tuos refufcitatus [vel refufcitata, vel refufcitati, &c.] refpiret. Per Chriftum Dominum noftrum. Refp. Amen.

Secundum Responforium.

Libera me Domine, de morte æterna, in die illa tremenda; quando cæli movendi funt & terra; dum veneris judicare feculum per ignem.

Verf. Tremens factus fum ego & timeo, dum difcuffio venerit, atq; ventura ira. Quando Cæli movendi funt & terra.

Verf. Dies illa, dies iræ, calamitatis & miferiæ, dies magna & amara valde. Dum veneris judicare feculum per ignem.

Verſ. *Requiem æternam dona eis Domine ꝫ Et lux perpetua luceat eis.*

Et repetitur Reſponſorium.

Libera me Domine de morte æterna, in die illa tremenda; quando Cœli movendi ſunt & terra, Dum veneris judicare ſæculum per ignem.

Kyrie eleiſon.

Chriſte eleiſon.

Kyrie eleiſon.

Pater noſter, &c.   Secreto.

Verſ. *Et ne nos inducas in tentationem.*

Reſp. *Sed libera nos a malo.*

Verſ. *A porta inferi.*

Reſp. *Erue Domine animam ejus.*

Verſ. *Requieſcat in pace.*

Reſp. *Amen.*

Verſ. *Domine exaudi orationem meam.*

Reſp. *Et clamor meus ad te veniat.*

Verſ. *Dominus vobiſcum.*

Reſp. *Et cum ſpiritu tuo.*

Oremus.

DEus cui proprium eſt miſereri ſemper & parcere; te ſupplices exoramus pro anima famuli tui N. quam hodie de hoc ſæculo migrare juſſiſti; ut non tradas eam in manus inimici, neꝙ obliviſcaris in finem ſed jubeas eam a ſanctis Angelis ſuſcipi, & ad patriam Paradiſi perduci; ut quia in te ſperavit & credidit, non pœnas *inferni sustineat, sed gaudia sempiterna possideat. Per Christum Dominum nostrum.*

Resp. *Amen.*

Tertium Responsorium.

In Paradisum deducant te Angeli; in tuo adventu suscipiant te Martyres, & perducant te in civitatem sanctam Hierusalem. Chorus Angelorum te suscipiat, & cum Lazaro quandam paupere æternam habeas requiem.

Kyrie eleison.

Christe eleison.

Kyrie eleison.

Pater noster, &c.　　　　Secreto.

Vers. *Et ne nos inducas in tentationem;*

Resp. *Sed libera nos a malo.*

Vers. *A porta inferi.*

Resp. *Libera Domine animam ejus.*

Vers. *Requiescat in pace.*

Resp. *Amen.*

Vers. *Domine exaudi orationem meam.*

Resp. *Et clamor meus ad te veniat.*

Vers. *Dominus vobiscum.*

Resp. *Et cum spiritu tuo.*

Oremus.

Fac, quæsumus Domine, hanc cum servo tuo defuncto (vel famula, vel famulis, &c.) misericordiam, ut factorum suorum in pœnis non recipiat vicem, qui tuam in votis tenuit voluntatem. ut sicut hic *cum vera fides junxit fidelium turmis, ita illic cum tua miseratio socies Angelicis choris. Per Christum Dominum nostrum.*

Resp. *Amen.*

Ver. *Requiem æternam dona ei Domine:*

Resp. *Et lux perpetua luceat ei.*

Ver. *Requiescat in pace.*

Resp. *Amen.*

Ver. *Anima ejus & animæ omnium fidelium defunctorum per misericordiam Dei requiescant in pace.*

Resp. *Amen.*

The Litanies for the Faithful Departed.

Which, (according to the fifth fore-going Rule) are to be recited upon each first Monday of the Month, in the head-Oratory, in the Procession there and then made for the relief of the Dead.

LOrd! have mercy upon us.

Christ! have mercy upon us.

Lord! have mercy upon us.

Christ! hear us,

O Christ! mercifully hear us

O God, the Father of Heaven !
  Have mercy on the Faithful departed.
O God, the Son, Redeemer of the
  World !
  Have mercy on the Faithful departed.
O God the Holy Ghoſt !
  Have mercy on the Faithful departed.
O ſacred Trinitie, one God !
  Have mercy on the Faithful departed.

Holy *Mary* !
Holy Mother of God !
Holy Virgin of Virgins !
Holy *Michael* !
All ye holy Angels and Archangels !
St. *John* Baptiſt !
St. *Peter* !
St. *Paul* !
St. *John* !
All ye holy Apoſtles and Evange-
  liſts !
St. *Stephan* !
St. *Lawrence* !
All ye holy Martyrs !
St. *Gregory* !
St. *Ambroſe* !
All ye holy Biſhops and Confeſſors !
St. *Mary Magdalen* !
St. *Catherine* !
All ye holy Virgins, and Widows !

Pray for the Faithful departed.

All ye Saints of God, intercede for the
  Faithful departed.

Be Propitious.   Spare them O Lord.
Be Propitious.   Hear them O Lord.
From all Evill,
From your Anger,
From the power of the Devil,
From the Flame of Fire,
From the Land of the shadow of
  Death,
By your immaculate Conception,
By your Nativitie and Circumci-
  sion,
By your most bitter Passion,
By your most sacred Wounds,
By your most precious Bloud,
By your most cruel and shameful
  Death,
By the multitude of your Mercies,

Deliver them, O Lord.

We Sinners, Beseech you to hear us.
Who gave to *Mary* Pardon, and to
  the Thief Paradise,
That you will vouchsafe to free our
  Parents, Kindred, Friends, and
  Benefactors from their punish-
  ment.
That you will vouchsafe to deliver
  all the faithful departed from
  eternal Damnation.
That you will be pleased to com-
  pleat their desired happiness,
That the Quires of Angels may
  comfort them,

We beseech you to hear us.

That the Patriarchs and Prophets may succour them.

That the glorious squadron of the Apostles may receive them.

That the triumphant Army of the Martyrs may encompass them.

That the holy Troop of the Confessors, may conduct them.

That the joyful Company of Virgins, may assist them,

That you, (O merciful Lord Jesu!) will give them the sight of your sweet countenance,

That you will place them on your right hand, in the company of your Elect,

That you will have mercy upon those departed Souls, which have no particular intercessors upon earth.

That you will vouchsafe to pity, spare and pardon all them of our Confraternity and Association.

O Son of God! the Fountain of Piety.

O Son of God! the King of Majesty.

Lamb of God! who takest away the sins of the World,
    Give them Rest.

We beseech you to hear us.

Lamb of God which takest away the
fins of the World,
Give them reft.
Lamb of God which takest away the
fins of the World,
Give them eternal reft.
Chrift hear us,
O Chrift, mercifully hear us.
Our Father, &c.
Ver. And lead us not into temptation.
Anf. But deliver us from evil.
Ver. Give unto them, O Lord, eternal
Reft.
Anf. And let your perpetual light
fhine upon them.
Ver. From the gates of Hell,
Anf. Deliver their Souls, O Lord.
Ver. Let them reft in peace.
Amen.
Lord, hear my prayer.
Anf. And let my cry come unto you.
Ver. Our Lord be with you.
Anf. And with thy Spirit.

Let us pray.
1. *On the day of the Death, or the
Anniverfary.*

O God ! whofe property it is, evermore to fpare and to have mercy :
We moft humbly befeech you for the

Soul of your Servant (*N.*) which you have called out of this world : that you will be graciously pleased, not to deliver it into the hands of the enemy, nor perpetually to forget it ; but that you will command your holy Angels to receive it, and conduct it to the heavenly Countrey : That since it hath hoped and beleeved in you, it may not suffer the infernal punishments , but may possess eternal happiness; Through Christ Jesus our Lord.

Anf. Amen.

2. For all the Faithful departed.

O God the Creator and Redeemer of all the Faithful ; pardon (we beseech you,) the sins of all your Servants ; and grant, that they may obtain your divine mercy, by these our pious prayers and supplications. Who livest and reignest for evermore.

Anf. *Amen.*

3. For our Brethren, Kindred, and Benefactors.

O God ! the giver of Pardon, and the lover of humane salvation ! We

Brethren of our Congregation, to our Kinsfolks, and to our Benefactors, who are departed out of this world, (by the intercession of the ever Blessed Virgin *Mary* and all your Saints,) that they may come to the fellowship of eternal felicitie. Through our Lord Jesus, Christ.

Ans. *Amen.*

The manner of officiating for the Dead.

The Priest sprinkles the Hearse with Holy water, saying,

The Anthem.

IF you, O Lord ! shall observe iniquities ; Lord *!* who shall sustain it ?

Then he recites the Psalm, 129.

From the depths I have cried to you, O Lord : Lord, hear my voice.

Let your ears intend to the voice of my supplication,

If you, O Lord ! shall observe iniquities : Lord ! who shall sustain it ?

Because with you there is propitiation ; and for your Law I have expected

My soul hath expected in your word: my soul hath hoped in our Lord.

From the morning watch even till night, let Israel hope in our Lord.

Because with our Lord there is mercy: and with him plentiful redemption.

And he will redeem Israel from all his iniquities.

Vers. Give them, O Lord! eternal rest.

Ans. And let perpetual light shine unto them.

The first Response.

Succour them, O ye Saints of God! meet them O ye Angels of our Lord! Receiving [this or] their Souls, and offering [it or] them up in the fight of the most High.

Vers. Let Christ who called [thee or] them, receive [thee or] them; and let the Angels conduct [thee or] them into the bosom of *Abraham.*

And it is repeated.

Receiving their Souls, and offering them up in the fight of the most High.

Vers. Give them, O Lord! eternal rest.

Ans. And let eternal light shine unto them.

Offering them up in the fight of the most High.

Our Father, &c, *In secret.*

Verf. And lead us not into temptation.

Anf. But deliver us from evil.

Verf. From the gate of Hell.

Anf. Deliver their Souls, O Lord.

Verf. Let them rest in peace.

Anf. Amen.

Verf. Lord, hear my Prayer.

Anf. And let my cry come unto thee.

Let us Pray.

ABsolve, (we beseech you, O Lord!) the Souls of your servants, from all the bands of their sins; that in the glory of the Resurrection, they may breath amongst your Saints and Elect; through our Lord Jesus Christ.

Anf. Amen.

The second Response.

Deliver me, O Lord! from eternal death, in that fearful day, when as the Heavens and the Earth are to be moved; whilst you shall come to judge the world by fire.

Verf. I become trembling and fearful, when the enquiry shall come, and the future anger. When the Heavens and the Earth shall be moved.

Verf. That day, is the day of anger, the day of calamity and of misery, a day,

which is great and very bitter; whilst
you shall come to judge the world by
fire.

Verf. Give them, O Lord! eternal
rest: And let perpetual light shine unto
them.

And the Refponfe is repeated.

Deliver me, O Lord! from eternal
death, in that fearful day, when as the
Heavens and the Earth are to be moved;
whilst you shall come to judge the
world by fire.

Lord! have mercy upon them.
Christ! have mercy upon them.
Lord! have mercy upon them.
Our Father, &c.   *In fecret.*
Ver. And lead us not into temptation.
Anf. But deliver us from evil.
Verf. From the gate of hell.
Anf. Deliver their souls, O Lord.
Verf. Let them rest in peace.
Anf. Amen.
Verf. Lord! hear my Prayer.
And let my cry come unto thee.

Let us Pray.

O God! whose property it is, evermore to spare and to have mercy:
We most humbly beseech you for the
souls of your servants, which you have
called out of this world; that you will

be gracioufly pleas'd, not to deliver them into the hands of the enemy, nor perpetually to forget them; but that you will command your holy Angels to receive them, and conduct them to the heavenly Countrey: That fince they have hoped and beleeved in you; they may not fuffer the infernal punifhments, but may poffefs eternal happinefs; Through Chrift Jefus our Lord.

Anf. Amen.

The third Refponfe.

Let the Angels lead them into Paradife, let the Martyrs receive them coming, and let the Saints conduct them into the holy City Jerufalem. Let the Quires of Angels receive them; and with poor *Lazarus,* let them enjoy eternal reft.

Lord! have mercy upon them.
Chrift! have mercy upon them.
Our Father, &c.   *In fecret.*
Ver. And lead us not into temptation.
Anf. But deliver us from evill.
Verf. From the gate of Hell.
Anf. Deliver their fouls, O Lord.
Verf. Let them reft in peace.
Anf. Amen.
Verf. Lord I hear my Prayer.
Anf. And let my cry come unto thee.

Let us Pray.

SHew this mercy, (we beseech you, O Lord!) to your departed servants; that they may not be punished according to their deserts, who had the performance of your will in their desires: and that as the true Faith joyn'd them here to the company of believing Christians; so your mercy may associate them there to the Angelical Quires. Through Christ Jesus our Lord.

Ans. Amen.

Vers. Give them, O Lord! eternal rest.

Ans. And let perpetual light shine unto them.

Vers. Let them rest in peace.

Ans. Amen.

Vers. Let their Souls, and the Souls of all the faithful departed, through Gods Mercy, rest in peace.

Ans. Amen.

V   SECT:

SECTION XIV.

The practical manner of performing the Roman Stations, in order to gain the Indulgences both for the living and the dead.

1. BEgin with the Sign of the Cross, as formerly in all your other devotions and spiritual exercises.

2. Offer up your *Stations* for the generally recommended ends and intentions, in all the Concessions of Indulgences, specified in the preparatory prayer before the recital of the Rosary ; *O Lord, open my mouth*, &c. page. 104.

3. With an humble and penitent heart, make this following Act of Contrition; thereby to settle your soul in the state of Grace; which is a necessary condition for the gaining of all Indulgences.

An Act of Contrition out of our Book of the Christians daily Exercise.

O my Sovereign Creator, and sweet Redeemer ! humbly prostrate at the

feet of your dread Majesty: I acknowledge the multitude and greatness of the
crimes I have committed against your
divine goodness. I acknowledge them,
O my gracious Lord God, with all possible shame and confusion; and I abhor
them with as much sense of sorrow, as
my poor heart is capable of.

Yea, my good God! It most heartily
grieves me to have so heinously offended you: not only by reason of the benefits which I have received from your
bounty, and abused by my ingratitude;
though I have just cause to be exceedingly afflicted upon this consideration:

Nor for having forfeited my right and
title to Heaven, and eternal felicity;
though I make my earnest sute to your
throne of mercy, that it may be again
restored unto me:

Nor for having deserved Hell and e-
ternal punishments; though I conjure
your paternal clemency to deliver me
from them:

But principally and (as neer as I can) only
because my crimes are displeasing, op-
posite, and offensive to your infinitely
amiable goodness; which meerly for
its own sake ought to be most sincerely,
affectionately and gratefully honoured
and obeyed by all your creatures, al-

though they could neither hope for any recompence, nor should dread any punishment.

In testimony of this my true sorrow, I here protest in your presence, (O my God!) that were all the felicities of heaven annihilated, and the fires of hell extinguished; so that there were no other good expected by serving you, than the sole rendering of my due love, gratitude and obedience; nor any other evil incurr'd by not serving you, than the sole depriving you of your due honour; I would (and do even at this very instant) begin to love, honour, and serve your sacred Majesty, with as much fidelity, as my former excesses have had disloyaltie.

Give me pardon (O merciful Maker!) for my past sins and impieties; and grace to amend for the future: and though I am most unworthy to have my prayers heard, or my petitions granted; because I am so enormous an offender: yet (O merciful Father!) look upon your meek Son *Jesus*, whose precious blood I present unto you; and beg for his dear sake, that you will be propitious to me a miserable and wretched Sinner.

4. Whilst you vocally recite the

Paters and *Aves*; you may mentally re-flect upon some of the fifteen Mysteries, as they are set down in the *Rosary* of the sacred *Name of Jesus*; dividing the same into *three days Stations,* after this manner.

Upon the first day, meditate upon the five Mysteries of our Blessed Redeemers Life; to wit,

1. Christs Incarnation, reciting five Paters and five Aves,: and then adding these words: O Jesu Christ, the Son of *David,* have mercy upon us; [*and when you intend your Stations for the benefit of the dead, say furthermore*] and upon the souls suffering in Purgatory.

2. His Nativity.

Five Paters and five Aves, O Jesu Christ, &c.

3. His Circumcision.

Five Paters and five Aves, O Jesu Christ, &c.

4. His finding in the Temple.

Five Paters and five Aves. O Jesu Christ, &c.

5. His Baptism.

Five Paters, and five Aves. O Jesu Christ, &c.

Upon the second day, meditate upon the five mysteries of our Blessed Redeemers Death and Passion; to wit,

1. Our Saviours washing his Disciples Feet.

Five Paters and five Aves. O Jesu of Nazareth, King of the Jews, have mercy upon us; and upon the souls suffering in Purgatory.

2. His Prayer in the garden.

Five Paters and five Aves. O Jesu.

3. His apprehension by *Judas*.

Five Paters and five Aves, O Jesu,

4. His carrying of the Cross.

Five Paters and five Aves, O Jesu.

5. His descent into Hell.

Five Paters and five Aves, O Jesu.

Upon the third day, meditate upon the five Glorious Mysteries of our Blessed Redeemer; to wit,

1. Christs Resurrection.

Five Paters and five Aves, O Jesu Christ, the Son of the living God, have mercy upon us, and upon the souls suffering in Purgatory.

2. His Ascension.

Five Paters and five Aves, O Jesu Christ, &c.

3. His sending the Holy-Ghost.

Five Paters and five Aves, O Jesu Christ, &c.

4. The Crowning of the Virgin *Mary*, and the Saints.

Five Paters and five Aves. O Jesu

5. The coming to judgement.

Five Paters and five Aves, and one Creed. O Jesu Christ, &c.

Glory be to the Father, and to the Son, and to the Holy Ghost:

As it was in the beginning, is now, and ever shall be, world without end. Amen.

An application of the Indulgence of the Stations to the Souls in Purgatory.

O Sweet *Jesu*! the dear and loving Bridegroom of the souls suffering in Purgatory: Give unto them (we beseech you) all that can be granted and given to us by the performance of these Stations: and let them (through your mercy and favour) feel the effects of the Plenary Indulgence, which we (relying upon the infinite treasure of your merits, upon the immense price of your blood, and upon the power of your Vicar upon earth) hope and have endeavoured to obtain in their behalf.

In particular, Deliver (O all-powerful Lord, and all-merciful Saviour!) from that dismal prison, and transfer into the liberty of your heavenly Paradise, the soul of our departed friend. *N.* &c.

And in case this Soul, for which we now most humbly crave your mercy, stands in no need of this our desired succour; be you pleased (O compassionate Lord!) to look in mercy upon the Souls:

1. Of our Parents, Kindred, Friends, Benefactors.

2. Of such as have been most charitable in praying for the departed.

3. Of such as are left uncomforted, unremembred, unprayed for.

4. Of such as suffer most, or who should (according to your justice) remain longest in torments.

5. Of such as are in the first and next place to be released.

6. Of such as most loved *Jesus, Mary, and Joseph.*

7. Of such as suffer there upon our occasion.

8. And lastly: Look in mercy (we beseech you,) upon our own poor souls, as if they were already departed out of our bodies: We beg of you (O blessed Jesu!) by the blood and water, which gushed forth of your wounded side and heart, in your bitter Passion; to pity us even at this present, and to permit us to advance here the payment for such punishments as we should hereafter pay in Purgatory.

Prayers for the dead; to Jesus,
Maria, Joseph.

JESUS.

O Jesu! the Saviour of our souls, whose inclination to do good to poor mankind, is so great, that you often press him to ask, and promise to grant his petitions: receive I beseech you this Prayer, which I most humbly present to your Throne of mercy, in behalf of [this my departed Brother or Sister] the souls suffering in Purgatory.

Remember, (O most compassionate Redeemer!) that it is a thing bought with your bloud, designed to your glory, intended to be a coheir with you in your heavenlie Kingdom. Look upon it (sweet *Jesu* !) as a noble conquest of your Cross, and the sacred Trophee torn by your power out of the Devils clutches; and, as such a thing afford it some solace in its sufferings, and free it from those flames, fetters, and prisons, which hinder it from enjoying that glorie, whereunto your mercy hath predestinated it, which your Passion hath purchased, and which your goodness hath prepared for it.

If the tears of *Mary* and *Martha* did so pierce your tender heart, that they obtained the raising of their dead brother *Lazarus* out of his Sepulcher; be not less favourable and flexible (O dear Saviour!) to these my sighs, tears, and prayers, which I now pour forth before you, for the soul of my departed Brother (or Sister.) Speak only the word, (O all-powerful Redeemer!) *N, come forth of those flames*, and Purgatorie will render you a most prompt obedience, and the delivered soul will eternallie magnifie your mercies.

M A R I A.

I most humblie salute you Great Queen of Heaven and Earth, Glorious Mother of Jesus, Powerful Advocatrix of mankind, and Compassionate Comforter of the afflicted! these blessed Titles imbolden me your unworthy servant to beg your assistance for the poor soul [of my departed Brother or Sister] now suffering, (as I probablie both fear and hope,) in the place of Purgatorie; and to petition you that you will be pleased to employ the power, the priviledge and the friendship you have with your dear Son Jesus in his behalf, and for his release, comfort and pardon.

O great and glorious Virgin Mother! consider this suffering soul, as by your Son redeemed, and by your self beloved; and since you have interest in the salvation and joy of the souls purchased by the price of your Sons precious bloud; take pity upon his soul, longing to behold your Son and your self in your glorie, and to sing forth your praises with the blessed Saints for all eternitie.

JOSEPH.

O faithful Steward of Gods sacred Familie, great and glorious St. *Joseph!* permit me to make my most humble addresses to you, in behalf of this poor soul suffering in the flames of Purgatory. It burns with an ardent desire to enjoy God, and to behold him in his heavenlie glorie; but the decree of the divine justice detains it from this desired happiness: be you therefore pleased, (O just man!) to interpose your pious intercession for the cancelling, or (at least) for the moderation of this severe Edict.

You formerlie freed *Jesus* and *Mary* from *Herod's* crueltie; free now this child of *Jesus* and *Mary* from the pains of Purgatorie; and obtain for him a you and your dear spouse *Mary*, praise, honour and enjoy *Jesus*, for all eternitie. *Amen.*

A ioynt Oblation and Prayer, to JESUS, MARIA, JOSEPH.

O Created Trinitie! who whilst you lived upon Earth, loved, served, and honoured the increated Trinitie sincerelie, faithfullie, inceflantlie: and who now reigning in Heaven; behold, adore, and enjoy the same divine Trinity, purelie, perfectlie, eternallie!

O admirable, amiable, and honourable Trinitie, *Jesus, Maria, Joseph!* receive the Trinitie of powers, which is in my poor foul, my Underftanding, my Will, my Memorie; to glorifie you, in contemplation of that high and holy Trinitie of the divine perfons, the Father, Son, and Holy Ghoft.

O *Trinitie!* fo lovelie in your felves, fo loving to mankind, and fo defirous of my falvation! affift me in loving you, help me to honour you, and efficaciouflie procure the falvation of my Soul.

To this end, O *Jesu my Saviour!* Present your facred Wounds to your Eternal Father, and the precious Blood you poured forth in your Paffion for my

O *Mary*, *my Mother* ! Discover your maternal breasts unto him, and mind him of the Virginal milk ; wherewith you suckled his coeternal *Son*, the Word Incarnate.

O *Joseph*, *my Patron*! Shew him your hands and offer him the *Sweat* of your brows; whereby you charitablie contributed to the corporal nourishment of *Jesu* and *Mary*.

O compassionate Trinitie, *Jesus*, *Maria*, *Joseph*! Be you joyntly pleased to sanctifie my Thoughts, to purifie my Words, to perfect my Actions; that so I may be agreeable to the glorious Trinitie, Father, Son and Holy Ghost: And let me be so happy both in life and death, in time and eternitie, as to belong to *Jesus*, *Maria*, and *Joseph*.

Gloria, laus, & honor,
Iesu, Maria, atque Joseph.

FINIS.

THE CONTENTS

Of this Book,

Iesus, Maria, Ioseph.

The Contents.

SECT. IV.

SECT. V.

SECT. VI.

The Contents.

SECT. VII.

SECT. VIII.

SECT. IX.

The Contents.

Several

The Contents.

SECT. XII.
JOSEPH:

OR, Devotions to St. Joseph, the Glorious Bridegroom of Mary, and reputed Father of Jesus. 219

The Contents.